MIDNIGHT
AT THE
MANSION

By Steven K. Smith

MyBoys3 Press

To Double A,
My newest reader and story buddy

MIDNIGHT
AT THE
MANSION

CHAPTER ONE

L unch was on Sam's mind as he walked with Caitlin past the black bear habitat. It was barely ten in the morning, but he was regretting not refilling his cereal bowl at breakfast. Even so, he was glad not to be the black bear's lunch. He watched it stroll across a trickling stream, splashing at the water with a giant paw.

Bears made Sam nervous, so he was glad when he and Caitlin moved on to the birds of prey area, another of the wild animal exhibits at Maymont, a former estate that was now a huge park in the city of Richmond.

"You know what I don't like about Benjamin Franklin?" said Caitlin, as they approached a large, wooden sign shaped like a bird's nest.

Sam raised an eyebrow. What did Ben Franklin have to do with anything? "Um…his weird glasses?"

Caitlin turned to Sam with a confused look. "I love his glasses…"

"Okay, what don't you like about Ben Franklin?" It was pointless to resist. Even though she was a girl, Caitlin was one of Sam's best friends in the whole fifth grade. She knew just about everything, but she also made sure you knew she knew it.

"He wanted our national bird to be the turkey!" Caitlin huffed, throwing her arms up like she'd witnessed some great injustice.

Sam thought about that for a moment. "Not such a bad choice. I love turkey…in sandwiches…at Thanksgiving…" His stomach rumbled again at the thought.

Caitlin frowned. "Exactly. Something you eat is probably not appropriate for the national bird."

Maybe she did have a point. They reached the open-air pen containing a pair of bald eagles.

"Look at them!" exclaimed Caitlin. "Aren't they amazing?"

Sam nodded. They sure were. He couldn't stop staring at their sharp beaks and white-feathered heads. He'd seen pictures of bald eagles so many times on dollar bills and other United States symbols that they seemed common, but now, being only a few feet away from the real thing was pretty sweet.

"See how intelligent they look? I wonder what they're thinking," said Caitlin.

Sam's stomach grumbled loudly.

Caitlin giggled. "I know what you're thinking."

He frowned and squinted to get a better look through the wire mesh. A dart of brown in the corner of the cage caught his attention. "That one's probably thinking about how many seconds to wait until he eats that mouse. Not a very smart mouse to wander into an eagle's cage."

"A mouse? Where?"

Sam pointed over to the corner of the cage just as the eagle spread its great wings. With a single flap, it swooped to the ground, grabbing the critter in its talons.

"Ahh!" shrieked Caitlin.

"Wow," Sam muttered, excited by the action. "I think he heard us say 'mouse.'"

"That's disgusting," said Caitlin, turning away. "Poor little mouse."

"That's just what eagles eat," said Sam.

"Just because something's true doesn't mean I need to think about it," she replied over her shoulder.

"Gosh, you don't have to be so squeamish about it," answered Sam. He'd been so caught up in watching the eagle and the mouse that he hadn't noticed the man who had walked up beside them until now.

"Quite something, aren't they?" the man said without taking his eyes off the birds. He was about

Sam's dad's age and wore glasses. A puff of black hair stuck out from under the bill of his brown, baseball-style hat.

"Uh, yeah, they are," Sam answered, realizing that the man was talking to them. He wasn't supposed to talk to strangers, but he also didn't want to be rude. He didn't know who this guy was, but he seemed okay. It wasn't like he was offering them candy or anything.

The man turned and smiled at them. "The eagle has always been a symbol of strength, all the way back to Roman times."

"It has?" said Caitlin.

Sam chuckled. It wasn't often that Caitlin was caught not knowing a fact about something.

The man nodded. "It became our national symbol back in 1782 when it was placed on the Great Seal. However, there were some who wanted a different bird."

"Benjamin Franklin!" shouted Caitlin. She gave Sam a smug grin, happy to show her knowledge off to someone else, especially a grownup. "He wanted the turkey."

"That's right," said the man. "Very impressive. You must be a bit of a historian yourself."

Caitlin beamed. "I'd like to be."

"She thinks she knows everything," added Sam.

"Do you work here?" asked Caitlin, casting a frown at Sam.

The man smiled. "Not exactly." He paused, seeming to consider his answer. "But I think of myself as someone on the side of history too. Our resources, like the eagles, need to be protected, you know. It wasn't long ago that these beautiful creatures were nearly wiped out. There were only a few hundred pairs of bald eagles left in the entire country, but laws were enacted to protect them, and now they're doing well again."

"Thank goodness," said Caitlin.

Sam nodded. He was glad the eagles were healthy again. They were too cool to go extinct.

The man's phone chirped on his belt. His expression changed when he glanced at the screen. Sam couldn't tell if it was worry or anger, but the man suddenly seemed nervous.

"Kids, I've gotta go. It was nice meeting you. Be careful where you go today." He pulled the brim of his hat down closer to his eyes and then quickly strode down the ramp from the bird exhibits.

Sam watched him break into a jog as he turned the corner, following the trail toward the river that ran beside the park.

"That was weird," said Caitlin.

"Yeah, where do you think he ran off to?"

"It must have been something to do with the message he got on his phone. He seemed nice, and he knew a lot about history."

"Maybe he's a killer," said Sam. "Every time he scores another victim, he visits a bird of prey to be near other predators."

Caitlin gave him a sideways glance and giggled. "You're crazy." She turned to leave. "You're starting to sound like Derek."

"Hey, now that is an insult," yelled Sam. His older brother could be a little goofy sometimes, a real pain most other times.

"Come on," said Caitlin. "We'd better go find that brother of yours. No telling what he's up to."

THEY FOLLOWED a trail that led across the rolling lawn toward the old mansion at the top of the hill. According to Sam's mom, a millionaire couple named the Dooleys donated the mansion and the entire one-hundred-acre estate to the City of Richmond when they died about one hundred years ago. Sam hadn't been there before, but Maymont was one of Caitlin's favorite places. When she invited him and Derek, excitedly describing the trails, gardens, wild animal exhibits, nature center, and the old mansion, it was hard to say no.

They climbed the sloping trail, surrounded by tall trees—oaks, or maples, or maybe sycamores. Caitlin would probably know but he wasn't about to ask her. As they approached one group of trees, Sam heard a familiar voice call his name. He looked around but didn't see anyone.

"Look, up there!" Caitlin pointed up into one of the tallest trees.

Sure enough, Sam's brother, Derek, was perched on a large branch forty feet in the air. He wore an orange helmet and a shoulder harness that was attached to a cable and pulley. Sam followed the wire down to the ground where two guys were holding support ropes. The name on their shirts was that of an outdoor adventure company in town.

Caitlin waved up to Derek in the tree. He was always wanting to climb on or jump off of something. Sam preferred to keep his feet closer to the ground.

"Watch this!" Derek yelled, stepping off the branch while grasping a handle that attached to the zip line. The men on the ground shifted their weight and held the support ropes tight as Derek flew along the zip line until he reached the stopping mechanism at the bottom of the cable and his feet gently touched down on the grass.

Sam's stomach turned upside down just watching, but he tried not to let it show. He'd decided that the fewer people who knew about his fear of heights, the less he would be teased about it.

"What do you think?" called Derek, unhooking himself from the ropes and harnesses.

"Wow!" said Caitlin. "That looks fun."

"Nice job," said Sam.

"I'll have to try that sometime," said Caitlin. "Is it scary?"

Derek put on a confident face and smiled wide. "Piece of cake. It's fun, like flying."

"Just for a few seconds," said Sam.

"Long enough to be fun, little brother." He nudged Sam in the arm. "You can go next if you want..."

Sam shook his head and looked away. "That's okay."

Derek laughed and turned to Caitlin. "Sam's a little bit chicken of heights."

Sam felt his cheeks burn red. He slugged Derek in the shoulder. "Shut up, I am not. I just don't feel like it." Sam took a deep breath, trying to count to ten. That's what Mom told him to do when Derek got him worked up, which was a lot.

Caitlin rolled her eyes. She walked across the grass toward a steep hill that sloped down behind the mansion, staring down the hill. "Come on," she called over her shoulder. "I want to see the gardens."

"That's a good idea," said Sam.

"I can go let the rope guys know you'll be back after you visit the chicken coop, Sam," Derek cackled.

Sam shot him an evil stare and started counting again. Staying relaxed around Derek was a full-time job.

"What?" Derek laughed. "What did I say?"

Caitlin led the way down a narrow stone path that cut through a grove of trees on the steep hill behind the mansion. The trail opened amongst an outcropping of large rocks that formed one side of a shaded garden. They all stopped and stared at a gentle waterfall flowing over the rocks beside them.

"I love this part," said Caitlin.

"Wow," said Sam. He felt like he'd stepped into a picture from a magazine. This secluded section was like another world compared to the rest of the park. "What is this place?"

"It's the Japanese Garden." Caitlin walked onto a delicate wooden bridge that rose up into an arch. "It's so beautiful, isn't it? This is my favorite part of the estate."

"Pretty cool," admitted Derek.

They followed the narrow dirt paths through the manicured gardens until they came to a small pond. A gazebo-like structure sat at one end, and in the middle, a dozen round stepping-stones connected to the opposite shore. Sam had never seen stones like these. They were flat on top and as big as truck tires. He stepped slowly from one to another, careful to keep a stone's distance behind Derek, just in case his brother had any ideas of pushing him in.

As he reached the end of the stone bridge, one eye on Derek, a large, orange streak moved past him in the water. "What was that?" he said, a bit more nervously than he would have liked.

Caitlin smiled, pointing into the water. "They're koi fish, Sam. It's a large Japanese koi pond."

Derek bent over laughing. "You should have seen your face. You thought you were a goner. They're a little small for sharks, Sam."

"I knew that," said Sam, brushing past his brother. He leapt onto the dirt path, looking back into the pond from the shore. The watermelon-sized fish were all through the water—some orange, some white, and others were a mix of both.

While Sam was staring at the colorful fish, a commotion sounded from the hill by the mansion. He looked up to see a man running toward the pond at full speed. He leapt over a bush, plowing through the middle of the gardens in a huge hurry. He was heading directly toward Sam on the shore of the pond. Sam recognized him as the man they'd talked to by the eagles' nest.

Sam dodged to his right to make way, but the man dodged the same direction. They crashed together, toppling onto the ground at the edge of the pond.

CHAPTER TWO

"Oomph!" groaned Sam, as the man sprawled next to him.

"Are you all right?" the man asked, quickly sitting up in the grass.

Sam wiggled his arms and legs. Everything seemed to be working. Thankfully the large man had missed landing on top of him. "I think so..." he answered slowly.

The man stared at Sam with faint recognition. A desperate, fearful expression filled his eyes. Sam noticed a smear of blood on the man's shirt collar. What was going on here?

Before Sam could ask anything more, a shout came from across the gardens and two more men burst out of the path and down the hill. They pointed at the man and Sam and began running toward them.

"Save the eagles," the man whispered into Sam's ear then scrambled to his feet. Or at least that's what Sam thought he heard.

"What?" asked Sam, but the man had already darted around the edge of the pond. Sam watched him crash through the row of tall bamboo trees that lined the back of the park. He quickly climbed over a chain link fence in a graceful motion, landed, and sprinted off to the left. In a flash the other two men tore past Sam, following the first man over the fence and out of sight. As quickly as they had come, all three men were gone.

Sam's heart was racing. He tried to catch his breath.

Derek and Caitlin hurried over to where he still sat in the grass.

"Sam, are you okay?" asked Caitlin, bending down to help him up.

He slowly nodded his head. "I think so."

"What was that all about?" asked Derek. "Did you trip that guy?"

Sam frowned, shaking his head.

"That was the man we talked to near the eagles, wasn't it?" asked Caitlin.

"Yeah," said Sam. "But I don't know who the other two were." He bent down to brush off his shorts.

"Looked like he was in trouble," said Derek.

As Sam looked down, he noticed something shiny at the edge of the koi pond. "Look at that!" It was a phone. It must have fallen off the man when he crashed into him.

"Oh, man, bad luck for that guy. It's probably waterlogged," said Derek.

Sam fished it out of the water. If it still worked, it probably wouldn't for long. He turned it over and was surprised to see words on the screen. "It says something!" exclaimed Sam.

Derek and Caitlin crowded around him.

"What is it?" asked Derek.

"Buyer coming...Dooley mansion," Sam read slowly.

"Dooley mansion?" asked Derek. "What's that?"

With an exasperated look, Caitlin pointed up the hill. "It's right here at Maymont, Derek."

"Oh, right. I knew that."

Sam scrolled down using the buttons on the phone. There was more. "Midnight...8-10," he said out loud.

"Midnight, eight to ten?" repeated Derek. "What the heck is that supposed to mean? How could something be at midnight *and* from eight to ten? Those are two different times."

Caitlin leaned closer to the screen. "It says eight dash ten. Maybe it's the date. Midnight on eight ten. August tenth?"

Sam tried to think. "What's today's date?"

"August first," said Caitlin.

"So someone is going to buy the mansion up there in nine days at midnight?" asked Derek.

Sam shook his head. "That can't be right."

Derek shrugged his shoulders. "Well, how should I know? If that guy would have stuck around a little longer, we could have asked him."

Caitlin stared off at the bamboo shoots in front of the fence. "I wonder if he got away?"

"Who was he anyway?" asked Derek. "And who were those two guys chasing him?"

Caitlin explained how they had met him by the eagles. "He said he was a historian, I think."

"Well, he's history now," Derek said with a laugh. "I hope he got away. Those other guys looked dangerous."

Sam walked over to where the man had disappeared. He pushed through the tall bamboo trees until he came to the fence. Behind the fence was a dirt trail, followed by a section of water which he thought was a canal. Behind the canal were railroad tracks which were in front of the river. As he stared through the fence, a train's whistle blasted from around the corner and slowly chugged into view. Sam gulped at the sight of the train. He silently hoped that the man hadn't drowned in the river or been run over on the tracks.

Suddenly he remembered the words the man had

whispered as he ran off. He'd forgotten to tell the others. "Save the eagles!"

Derek and Caitlin looked up in surprise at Sam's shout. "You mean the Philadelphia Eagles?" said Derek. "It's not even football season, although they're not supposed to be very good this year."

Sam shook his head and explained again what the man had whispered.

"I think he meant the bald eagles, Derek," said Caitlin. "That's where we met him. It must be."

"But why would they need to be saved?" asked Sam. "We just saw them, they seemed fine."

Caitlin shrugged. "I don't know. Let's check on them on the way up to the mansion. We should tell somebody about this."

Sam stuck the man's phone in his pocket, and they walked around the back trail of the park to the animal exhibits. Everything seemed normal with the eagles; they were still there acting like eagles do. Since there was no immediate threat to the eagles, they marched up the hill across the wide lawn until they reached the mansion in the middle of the estate.

Groups of people strolled the grounds, and two little kids rolled in the grass, playing with balloons. A sign marked one of several smaller buildings as stables for the horses used in carriage rides and another was like a museum with old carriages and sleighs from the days of the Dooleys. It was hard to imagine living back then on a such a huge estate. Some rich people probably still did live in places like this, but not anyone Sam knew, that was for sure.

Sam looked up at the mansion. It was really too big and grand to be called a house. A brown-colored stone exterior led to a roof with a series of peaks, two of the corners cone-shaped like the kind on a castle. A large, covered porch wrapped around the first floor and extended into a roofed entranceway over the driveway like at a hotel.

The mansion reminded him of a haunted house from a commercial he'd seen for a scary movie. It was a cool place, but he imagined it would be pretty creepy to see in the dark. If the phone's message meant something would happen at midnight, he hoped it was wrong. But he had no intention of being there to find out.

"Do we just knock on the front door?" asked Derek.

"No," said Caitlin, "come around to the side, that's where they give tours." She pointed to stone steps leading down to a basement level.

"Have you been on a tour before?" asked Sam.

Caitlin shook her head. "Not that I can remember, but my mom has, and she told me about it. She came during the holidays when things were all decorated for Christmas. It sounded fun."

The three of them walked down the steps to the basement door. A sign said they should knock to be waited on, so Caitlin rapped on the door.

"May I help you?" an older woman answered, opening the door.

"We need to talk to someone in charge," said Derek.

"Are you looking to go on a tour?" the woman asked, looking around behind them. "With your parents, perhaps?"

Caitlin spoke up. "We just ran into a man who was being chased by the Japanese Gardens. We think he was in trouble."

"He ran into us, actually," said Derek.

Caitlin shushed him. Sam knew she preferred to be the one to do the talking to grownups. "He told us to save the eagles."

The woman nodded, seeming unimpressed. "Lots of people want to help save the eagles, dear, ever since they became endangered. They're right down the hill by the other animal habitats if you want to see them."

"But..." Sam tried to think of how to explain what had happened, but the words were all jumbled in his head. "There's a buyer coming to the Dooley Mansion at midnight."

"On August tenth!" said Derek.

"A buyer?" The woman's face turned sour. "A buyer for what?"

"We don't know," Caitlin admitted.

"Well, the park closes at eight this time of year, and we have no activities planned for the tenth. I'm afraid you must have gotten some bad information." She leaned closer to them. "Maybe your friend was playing a joke on you."

Sam shook his head. "He wasn't our friend. And it's true. We have his message." He pulled the phone from his pocket and held it up to the woman.

"I don't see anything, dear," said the woman.

Sam looked at the screen. It was blank. The water must have shorted out the electronics. He smiled weakly at the woman. "It was on there before, honest. The phone got wet and now it's not working."

"This is the Dooley mansion, isn't it?" said Derek.

The woman nodded. "That's right, built by Major James and Sallie May Dooley in 1893."

"But someone might be in danger," said Sam.

"That man…he might be hurt," Caitlin pleaded.

The woman glanced at her watch as another group of people walked up behind them. "Yes, well you'll have to excuse me now, our next group is arriving. If you'd like to come back for a scheduled tour, we'd love to have you."

"But what about the message?" asked Caitlin.

"Yeah, and the eagles?" said Sam.

"I think they'll be fine, children. Move along now." She waved them away from the door, motioning for the group to come in. All three sulked back up the basement steps and out onto the paved path that circled the mansion.

"This is really strange," said Caitlin, a puzzled expression on her face. "That man didn't seem to be fooling around. Did he look that way to you?"

Sam shook his head. "No way. You should have seen his face. He was scared."

"Well, there's not much more we can do about it now," Caitlin sighed. She pointed to the blank phone in Sam's hand. "All of our proof is gone."

Sam turned to talk to Derek, but he wasn't standing with them. "Derek?" Sam looked around. "Where'd he go?"

Caitlin pointed toward the basement entrance where they'd talked to the woman. Derek was standing in the back of a line of people filing into the building. He was grinning and motioning for them to join him.

CHAPTER THREE

"Oh, no," muttered Sam. Derek was always getting bright ideas to do things that didn't seem very smart. Sneaking onto the tour would definitely get them in trouble.

"What's he up to this time?" said Caitlin, heading toward Derek.

Sam sighed and reluctantly followed. When he reached his brother, Sam whispered, "What do you think you're doing?"

"We have to look for clues if we're going to figure out what's happening at the mansion." Derek nodded at the line. "What better way than on a tour?"

Sam shook his head and took Derek's arm to pull him away. "You have to pay to go on the tour. Did you bring any money?"

Derek shook his arm free. "No, but this is an emergency. You saw the message. We have to do something."

Sam looked to Caitlin for support, but she just shrugged. "He's kind of right. What if something terrible is going to happen? We can pay them back later. I'm sure they'd understand."

Sam thought about going to tell his mom. She was taking a pottery class over in the learning center on the other side of the estate. He didn't want to go on a tour. How long did they even last? He was still hungry and they were supposed to meet Mom at the entrance at lunchtime.

The line ahead of them started moving.

"Come on!" said Derek.

Sam groaned but followed, trying to look casual and blend in with the back of the line. He hid his face as they passed the visitors' desk in the downstairs level of the mansion. He didn't want to see the woman they'd spoken to before. He didn't like sneaking into things they weren't supposed to do or places they weren't supposed to go. Getting yelled at made him nervous. He looked up at Derek and wondered why he didn't seem to have the same problems.

They stood with the other tour members in a wide hall that opened into several different rooms. A guide said they could look around on their own for ten minutes before heading upstairs. The area was clean and orderly, but it was pretty plain and most of the rooms were small.

"Not much of a fancy mansion," Sam muttered. He'd thought it would be a little nicer than this.

Caitlin chuckled. "That's because this is the *below stairs* area. Didn't you read the sign?" She pointed to small placards with pictures and descriptions around the room. "This is where the servants worked to run the household. They were almost all African American and worked very hard to keep everything upstairs running smoothly for the Dooleys."

"How do you know all that?" asked Sam. The sign was too small to have told her that much. "I thought you haven't been on the tour before?"

Caitlin smiled. "My mom told me, but it also reminds me of a show my parents watch on TV about a big mansion like this, except that was in England."

Geez, that girl remembered everything.

They walked to the first room that was labeled "Butler's Room."

"I wonder if the butler's name was Alfred," said Derek.

Caitlin scrunched her eyebrows. "Alfred?"

"You know, like in Batman. Alfred was Bruce Wayne's butler."

"Except this really happened," said Sam. "It's not just a movie."

"Actually it was a comic book, then a TV show, then a movie."

Sam rolled his eyes. "Whatever."

Caitlin pointed to another sign in the room. "It says one of the butlers' names was William Dilworth. And look, after he worked here, he was the head waiter at The Jefferson!"

"Cool," said Sam. The Jefferson was an elegant, old hotel in downtown Richmond that they'd visited for a wedding on another of their adventures. It used to have real alligators living in the fountains in the lobby. Things had gotten pretty crazy while they were there, but that was a whole different story.

Sam continued through the hall, peeking into each room they came to. Besides the Butler's Room there was a kitchen, laundry, pantry, a cold room—which seemed to be like the refrigerator—furnace room, servants' room, and the wine cellar.

Sam wondered what it would be like to have a house full of servants. Pretty nice for the owners, but not so nice for the servants, he decided. It looked like they had to do a lot of work down here.

"Do you see any clues?" asked Derek.

Sam shrugged. He'd nearly forgotten that they were supposed to be looking for clues. But what were they even looking for? Everything seemed normal, but what would "not normal" even look like? Sneaking into the mansion was a dumb idea. There wasn't anything here to tell them about buyers coming for the eagles on August tenth. Derek just liked the thrill of doing something they weren't supposed to do. Sam was tempted to turn around and head out.

When he had almost decided to leave, people from the tour started heading upstairs, so the three of them followed until the whole group was assembled in a grand, open foyer near what appeared to be the front door. Upstairs, everything suddenly looked very different from the basement level. Now it made sense why so many workers were needed to keep things in order. Everything was ornately decorated—expensive-looking furniture, gold-colored curtains draped around the windows, marble sculptures on pedestals against the walls. And not a dust ball or bit of clutter was in sight. He supposed it was easier to keep clean since no one actually lived there. His mom was always harping on him and Derek to pick up their things because the house was a mess. Maybe if he had a squad of servants to help it might be easier to keep her happy.

"This place is huge," said Derek. "I wonder how many people lived here?"

The tour guide seemed to have overheard his question. She was an older lady with grayish hair up in a bun. She wore a thin white sweater and pants a color

Sam's mom would call salmon. The tag on her sweater said *Doris*.

Could she tell they were stowaways on the tour? The thought made Sam's stomach tighten, but Doris smiled like she was happy just to see kids paying attention.

"That's a good question," she answered. "Believe it or not, only James and Sallie Dooley lived here."

"What about their kids?" asked Caitlin.

Doris smiled again. "They never had any children, I'm afraid."

Derek whistled. "Too bad. This would be a sweet place to grow up."

"However," continued Doris, "the Dooleys were major contributors to the local children's hospital and St. Joseph's Orphanage. They cared about children a great deal."

The tour moved through the first floor rooms. Sam had never seen such a well-decorated house—sculptures, oriental rugs, huge mirrors, and fine china everywhere. He could only imagine how much damage he and Derek would cause if they lived here. It wouldn't be pretty.

"The Dooleys moved into this thirty-three-room mansion in 1893," explained Doris. "It was the grandest home in all of Richmond, complete with electric lighting, an elevator, three full bathrooms, and central heating. That might not seem like too much now-a-days, but over a hundred years ago, it was quite extravagant."

She led the group up a paneled wooden staircase to an upstairs hallway. Caitlin was just ahead of Sam. When they reached the bedrooms, she caught her breath. "Oh my goodness! Sam, you have to see this!"

Had Caitlin found a clue after all? Sam shouldered past her and entered what looked like a woman's bedroom. On the far side of the room, in a corner surrounded by windows, was a huge, white bird. It wasn't real, though. It was an enormous piece of furniture elaborately carved in the shape of a white swan, with a long curved neck and a wide feathered tail at the other end.

"What is it?" asked Sam. He wanted to ask what the giant bird statue had to do with the eagles, but Doris was close by.

"It's a bed," replied Caitlin, still staring wide-eyed. "See, the blue cushion in the middle is the mattress."

"That's right," said Doris. "Sallie Dooley adored swans, particularly because they choose a single mate for their lifetimes. Her husband had this bed made specially for her in New York. It's beautiful, isn't it?"

Caitlin nodded. "Sure is. I'd love to sleep in a bed like that. It's so…luxurious. I bet I'd dream of flying. Wouldn't you, Sam?"

"Uh, maybe..." Sam mumbled, forcing himself not to roll his eyes. Now, if the bed was shaped like a Lamborghini, that would be sweet.

"The other interesting thing about that bed," said Doris, "is that it wasn't originally here at Maymont."

Caitlin turned her head. "It wasn't? But I thought you said that it was Sallie Dooley's?"

"That's right, but originally it resided in the Dooleys' summer house, a magnificent palace called Swannanoa."

Sam chuckled. He suspected this was a trick Doris liked to play on visitors. A swan bed was one thing, but a whole palace? That had to be a joke. "Come on. Swannanoa? No one would name a palace that."

Again the guide nodded. "You might if you liked swans as much as Sallie Dooley did."

"Where is Swannanoa?" asked Caitlin, apparently believing the story. "Is it here in Richmond, too?"

Doris shook her head. "Swannanoa was the Dooleys' summer house. It's up on Afton Mountain, on the edge of the Blue Ridge Mountains, west of Charlottesville." She looked at her watch. "But I'm afraid we need to keep the tour moving. Let's walk into the next room, which was Major Dooley's study."

As they shuffled down the hall, Caitlin nudged Sam. "Are you thinking what I'm thinking?" she whispered.

"That it's dumb to name a palace after a swan?" called Derek from behind them. For once, his brother seemed to agree with him.

Caitlin frowned. "No. Think about the message. It said there were going to be buyers at the Dooley mansion. What if it didn't mean *this* mansion here at Maymont..."

Sam's face brightened. He saw what she meant. "Oh...you mean it could be their other mansion out on Afton Mountain?"

"Swannanoa," said Derek.

"Right," said Caitlin.

Sam thought about it for a moment. "It's possible, I guess."

Derek glanced back at the room with the swan bed. "I still think it's a stupid name."

Caitlin ran her hand along the decorative wood in the hallway. She had a wistful look in her eyes. "Swannanoa...it sounds like something in a dream, like it's up in the clouds."

Sam looked at her funny. Seeing that swan bed must have messed with her head.

"Do you think...that it's really a palace?" said Caitlin.

"Do they even have palaces anymore?" asked Derek.

Caitlin bit her bottom lip and turned her head like she was thinking hard. "Let's go home and think about it. I'll try to do some research on my computer."

As they turned the corner, Sam bumped into someone walking the other way. "Oh, sorry," he mumbled. He looked up into the face of the woman from the basement door.

She glanced down at him in surprise. "Just one minute, young man. Let me see your tour receipt."

"Run!" shouted Sam.

CHAPTER FOUR

"Come back here, children!" the woman called after them. "This is not a gymnasium! Stop!"

Caitlin and Derek followed Sam down the staircase, through the front foyer, and out the front door. They didn't slow down until they were across the grassy lawn in front of the stables.

Sam bent over with his hands on his knees, trying to catch his breath.

Caitlin started laughing. "Sam, you didn't have to run away. I was going to explain to her."

He grinned and tried to relax. "She surprised me. I didn't want to get in trouble."

"He's a little skittish," said Derek.

"You both followed me," said Sam.

Derek looked back at the mansion, his hands on his hips. "You know what this means, don't you?"

Sam tried to ignore the devilish grin on his brother's face. "That the Dooleys were really rich to have two mansions?"

Derek shook his head. "It means that we have to go to Afton Mountain and see Swannanoa."

Sam stood up straight. "No way."

"He's right, you know," agreed Caitlin. "If that message is true, then something bad is going to happen to the eagles on the tenth. We can't just sit around and let it happen."

"But the eagles are *here*, not at Swannanoa," said Sam. "It could just as easily mean Maymont."

"True," said Caitlin. "Let's think about it. And I'll do some research about Swannanoa."

"Yeah, but it sounds cool to go see a palace on a mountain, doesn't it?" said Derek. "Can't you try to be adventurous for a change, Sam?"

Sam frowned. "Living with you is plenty of adventure, trust me."

Caitlin laughed.

Derek patted Sam on the back and smiled. "Well then, just consider this part of the adventure, little bro."

* * *

WHEN THEY ARRIVED BACK HOME, after their mom dropped off Caitlin, Derek ran inside to show their dad a picture of him riding the zip line. They'd all decided not to tell their parents about what had happened until they could do more research. While Sam was still on the front porch, an enormous noise sounded from the yard next door.

"What is that?" he screamed to his mom, while he covered his ears from the noise. He looked over at his neighbor, Mr. Haskins' house. There was no telling what the kooky old man might be doing.

Mom shook her head and said something that Sam couldn't hear, so he stepped over to the fence between their yards and stared through the tree branches. Mr. Haskins was in his backyard, pushing some kind of machine. Sam cautiously climbed over the fence and walked up to the old man.

Mr. Haskins had big earmuffs on his head while pushing a giant, motorized blower machine across the grass. As he turned the machine for another pass, Mr. Haskins glanced up, stopping suddenly with a jump when he saw Sam. He patted his chest with his hand in surprise and bent over. For a second, Sam feared he'd scared the old man to death, but he was just turning the machine off.

"What are you trying to do?" Mr. Haskins stood up and yelled, much louder than usual. "Give me a heart attack?"

Sam tried to look friendly. "Sorry, Mr. Haskins."

"What's that you say?" the old man hollered, leaning forward with his eyebrows scrunched together.

Sam realized the earmuffs on Mr. Haskins' head were noise protection headphones. He pointed at his own head to signal him.

"Huh? What's wrong with your head, boy?"

Sam stepped forward and lifted the headphones off his neighbor's head.

"Oh...well, why didn't you tell me, boy?" He looked disgusted. "It's not nice to play tricks on an old man, you know."

Sam was about to argue his innocence, but he decided better of it. "What are you doing?" he asked instead. "Trying to blow the grass off your yard?"

Mr. Haskins waved his hand at the air like he was swatting a bug. "Aw, come on. I just got this grass to start growing back here, why would I blow it away?"

"Then what?" Sam looked around, wondering if he'd missed something obvious.

Mr. Haskins frowned. "It's for the leaves, Einstein. I'd have at least expected you to know that one, boy."

"But the leaves are still on the trees." Sam pointed above their heads at the branches, still flush with green. It would be at least a month before they started showing any hints of orange and yellow.

Mr. Haskins stared up like he'd never realized there were trees in his yard. "Oh, well of course they're still on the trees. But I'm getting ready for them." He patted the blowing machine. "This puppy blows over one hundred miles an hour. Those leaves'll never know what hit 'em."

"Oh," was all Sam could think to say. Mr. Haskins cared a little too much about his yard, although maybe old people didn't have much else to worry about, so it might be understandable.

"Sam, come on, the game's starting!" Derek called from their house.

Sam remembered that a big baseball game was coming on TV that afternoon. He'd been looking forward to it all week. "Coming!" he hollered, then turned back to Mr. Haskins. "I gotta go."

He took a few steps toward his house but tripped over a large gully on the edge of the grass. "Whoops. Sorry." He looked back to make sure Mr. Haskins wasn't mad. He always yelled at them for stepping in his flowerbeds, maybe this was something else to avoid.

"Good thing there aren't any fish in there or you'd have a wet foot."

"Fish?" Sam looked down at the hole. It didn't look like any fish would live in a gully in the grass.

"Sure, that used to be my koi pond, but not for probably..." the old man scratched his head, "oh, at least fifteen years by now. Too much work, I decided." He bent down and picked a weed. "Of course, now I got all this doggone grass to deal with. Maybe I should just make it one big fish pond!"

Sam's ears perked up. "You had a koi pond? We just saw one of those over at Maymont today, but a big one."

Mr. Haskins nodded. "Sure, I know it well. Back in the Japanese Gardens. Been there many times. Did you walk on the stepping stones?"

"Yeah, they were cool." Sam's mind jumped ahead to all they'd learned at the estate. "Hey, Mr. Haskins...do you know anything about a place called Swannanoa?"

Mr. Haskins looked down over his glasses. "What do *you* think, boy? I've only lived in this area my whole life."

"Have you been there?"

Mr. Haskins eased himself down into a wooden chair next to his deck. "I have. But it's been a while."

Sam sat next to him on the deck steps. "Is it really a palace?"

Mr. Haskins nodded. "Pretty fancy place. Gardens, towers, marble stairs, and an enormous stained glass window of Sallie Dooley."

Sam remembered that was the name of the lady with the swan bed. "Did you know her?"

"Who?"

"Sallie Dooley."

"Hah! Now how old do you think I am, boy? The Dooleys were before even *my* time. That place sat empty for years after the Dooleys died. One time, the Navy was going to turn it into a secret base to interrogate war prisoners."

Sam's ears perked up. "Really?"

"Yeah, but they never did," continued Mr. Haskins. "Then, for a long time, it was some mumbo jumbo science and philosophy retreat."

"Wow," said Sam. The science and philosophy thing sounded boring, but a secret Navy base was cool. "What is it now? Does someone live there?"

"Nah, not anymore, I don't think. Last I heard, it was mostly abandoned and had fallen into disrepair. A real shame, too."

"Why didn't they make it a park like Maymont?" asked Sam. If it was so amazing, he figured that would be a good way to take care of it.

"Dunno, boy. Sometimes things that make sense don't always happen. Takes a lot of scratch to keep up a place like that."

"Scratch?"

Mr. Haskins frowned and leaned forward in his chair. With one hand, he reached out and rubbed his thumb against his fingers. "Cash, boy. Fixing up a mansion is expensive."

Sam thought of another question. "Do they have bald eagles there?"

Mr. Haskins tilted his head back and stared at the sky. "Might be some in the trees up on Afton Mountain, if that's what you mean. It's pretty wooded, being part of the Blue Ridge, you know. There's plenty of black bear, lotta snakes too. Gotta be some eagles. They're making a comeback, I hear."

Sam's eyes opened wide at the sound of bears and snakes, but he tried to focus on the message and the eagles. "Do they keep them on the grounds at Swannanoa, like they do at Maymont? The bald eagles, I mean."

Mr. Haskins shook his head. "Don't think so. Like I told you, it's mostly abandoned."

"Sam! You're missing the game!" Derek called again from the house, louder this time.

Sam tried to force thoughts of eagles and Swannanoa out of his mind. He really wanted to see the ballgame. He stood up from the step.

"Thanks, Mr. Haskins. Good luck with your leaves."

The old man grunted. "Don't need luck, I've got my secret weapon." He pointed to his blower machine. "They haven't got a chance."

CHAPTER FIVE

After the ballgame and dinner, Derek challenged Sam to a Ping-Pong match. Dad had bought them a table for the basement at Christmas, and they had a lot of fun playing together before bedtime most nights. Dad was a champion player in his rec league in college, and he was teaching the boys how to play. Derek had caught on quickly and regularly beat Sam, but Sam was secretly counting down the days until he could beat his older brother and couldn't wait to see the look on his face.

After his latest defeat, Sam headed upstairs to get ready for bed. He stopped when he heard the sound of his mother's voice in the next room.

"I know. I can't believe it. We were just there."

He leaned his head around the doorframe, catching a glimpse of her talking on the phone.

"You're kidding," his mom continued. "Both of them? That's so sad. I love that place."

Sam listened on the other side of the doorway, trying to think of who she could be talking to. It could be Mr. Haskins, since Sam was just over there, but he didn't usually call on the phone. He just wandered over to chat or complain about whatever it was Sam and Derek had done wrong this time. Sam knew he shouldn't eavesdrop, but this sounded interesting.

"Hiding from someone?" said Derek, sneaking up behind him.

"Shh!" Sam motioned for him to be quiet. Derek leaned in behind him to catch a glimpse. "Spying on Mom now, are you?" he whispered. "How exciting can that be?"

Sam frowned and motioned for him to be quiet.

"Well, thank you for calling," said Mom. "Hopefully it will all work out in the end." She was walking toward them.

Sam pushed Derek back, scampering further into the hall, trying to look casual. Their mom came around the corner but stopped short when she saw them.

"Hey, Mom," said Derek. "Who was that?"

"What?" She looked surprised. "Oh...no one. I need to talk to your father. Have you seen him?"

"I think he's in his office," said Sam, unsure of why Mom would be acting so strangely. "Everything okay?"

She nodded but headed off looking preoccupied.

"What's that all about?" said Derek.

"Beats me," replied Sam. "But she looks worried about something."

Derek's phone buzzed in his pocket. He read something, then looked at Sam. "Uh...you need to call Caitlin."

"Why?"

"How should I know? I just got a message from Jack Corey saying that his sister told him you're supposed to call Caitlin." Derek shook his head. "When are Mom and Dad going to let you have your own phone? I'm not your personal secretary, you know."

"Be quiet," huffed Sam. Derek had finally convinced their parents to let him have a phone when he started middle school, and it quickly turned into one more thing for him to lord over Sam about being older.

Sam took the phone from the kitchen and punched in Caitlin's number as he walked upstairs to his bedroom. Why didn't she just call him herself? This was strange.

"Hello?"

"Hey, it's Sam. Did you want me to call you?"

"Yes! Thank goodness." It sounded like Caitlin was breathing fast.

"What's up? And why didn't you just call me yourself?"

"My mom just talked to your mom on the phone."

So that's who she was talking to. Sam tried to think about what Mrs. Murphy could have told his mom to make her seem so nervous. "What did she want?"

"It was about the eagles," said Caitlin.

Sam caught his breath. "Eagles? You mean the Maymont ones?"

"Exactly."

"Exactly what? What's wrong with them?" asked Sam.

"They're gone."

Had he heard her right? "Gone? Like, taken to a different park?"

"No," answered Caitlin. "Like gone, gone. As in stolen. As in missing."

Oh my gosh. It was just like the man had warned them. *Save the Eagles.*

"But there's more," said Caitlin. "Remember the man we talked to that jumped over the fence by the Japanese Gardens?"

Remember him? Sam touched his ribs. He was still a little sore from where the man had crashed into him at the koi pond. "Of course I do..."

"Well, apparently he was an undercover marshal for the National Park Service!"

"National Park Service?" repeated Sam. He'd never heard of marshals in the parks. He thought a marshal was someone who rode a horse in those old black and white movies. National parks had forest rangers or something, didn't they?

"And that's not the worst of it."

"It's not?" said Sam. "How could it be worse?"

Caitlin lowered her voice to a whisper. "You're not going to believe this."

"What?" said Sam, after she paused without saying anything. "What am I not going to believe?"

"I think he's dead."

Sam's heart felt like it stopped beating. "Dead?"

"I think so. Mom said he was missing, but I think she was trying not to scare me, since we were just at Maymont this afternoon and all. I didn't tell her we'd met him. That would have been too much for her, I think. She'd never let me out of the house. I bet it was those two guys who were chasing him that killed him. Did they look like killers to you?"

Sam tried to process what Caitlin had just told him. She was talking fast and there was a lot of information. What did it mean if that guy was dead? Why would anyone kill him?

"And I think they're calling in the FBI since he was a federal marshal," added Caitlin.

The FBI? This was crazy. How could a visit to Maymont turn into a robbery, murder, and calls to the FBI?

Caitlin interrupted him before he could finish his thought. "I've got to go, my mom's calling me. I'll talk to you later."

"Okay..."

"And Sam?"

"Yeah?"

"Be careful."

"Wait, what?" Sam asked, but she'd already hung up. What did she mean by that? He wondered if he might have been the last person the marshal talked to. Was he in danger now too?

Sam turned around, still thinking about the phone call, just as something flew at him, pelting him in the forehead. "Ahh!" he yelled.

"Nailed you!" shouted Derek, grinning mischievously on the other side of the room. A blue sponge ball rolled into the corner.

"Will you cut it out!" cried Sam, reaching for the ball. "What's the matter with you?" He whipped it back toward his brother, but it bounced off the doorway.

"Nice try," said Derek. "What did your girlfriend want?"

"Shut up." Sam felt his cheeks flush, despite trying not to let them. Derek always teased him about hanging out with Caitlin. They were just friends, but for some reason Sam let Derek's words bother him more than they should. Somehow his brother knew just what to say to get under his skin.

Sam tried to focus. "She called to tell me that it was *her* mom that our mom was talking to. The eagles at Maymont disappeared."

"What?"

Sam nodded. "But it's worse. The man that crashed into me might be dead."

Derek's smile faded. "Sam, even *I* don't joke about people dying. You always have to take things a little too far."

Sam frowned. "*I* always take things too far..." Was he kidding? Derek was the one who always took things too far.

Derek winked at him.

Sam tried to remember what they were talking about. "Listen, I'm serious. Caitlin just told me. Do you think it was those men who were chasing him? Could they really have killed him?"

Sam sat down at his desk, putting his head in his hands. He was sweating. "I think we should tell Mom and Dad. Maybe go to the police. Or the FBI." He explained what Caitlin had said about the man being a marshal.

Derek sat quietly for a moment on the bed. "You do have his phone. Maybe that could be evidence. Too bad it doesn't work anymore."

Sam had forgotten all about the phone. He opened the desk drawer he'd put the phone in when they got home. He looked at the screen. "Still dead."

"Let me see," said Derek, taking the phone out of its thin plastic case. He wiped a few remaining drops of water off on his shirt and blew into the holes. It was still blank. "Well, I guess it isn't really evidence if it's broken."

"Boys, time for lights out," their mom's voice called up the stairs.

Derek yawned and walked over to the doorway. "Let's tell Mom and Dad tomorrow. There's nothing anyone can do about it tonight."

Sam was about to argue when he forced back a yawn too. Maybe Derek was right. It had been a long day, and he was too tired to think anymore. "Okay." He set the phone down on the nightstand next to his bed. "But we'll definitely tell them tomorrow."

"Definitely."

Sam had a hard time falling asleep. He kept picturing the marshal's face as they tumbled to the ground together. His scared face. He wondered if the man was really a federal marshal. If he was, why would he be scared? Weren't marshals like the police? Wouldn't he be tough and have a gun?

Then Sam thought of the big men who had been chasing him. Maybe they had guns too. That could have been why he was running, or maybe the marshal had lost his. Sam shuddered again, thinking of how close he had been to all three of them. Even if the marshal was tough, he'd still likely be scared when being chased. Sam knew he certainly would be. Eventually he drifted off, but his dreams chased him all night.

When he opened his eyes, the room was still dark and he was sweating again. He wondered if he was still dreaming. He was usually a super sound sleeper, but he didn't feel rested at all. He peered over at the alarm clock on his dresser. 1:05 AM. He yawned and rubbed his eyes. It was the middle of the night. Why had he woken up?

Something buzzed next to him, a faint green glow on his nightstand. What was that? He leaned toward the glow then froze.

It was the phone.

The dead man's phone.

It was working, and something was lighting up the screen. He swallowed hard and picked it up. Maybe he *was* still dreaming. He didn't know if he really wanted to look at it. He leaned back against the headboard of his bed, blinking at the light from the screen in the darkness.

"Buyer coming - Dooley mansion. Midnight 8-10."
He let out a long breath. It was just the same message as

before. But then he saw the edge of an image at the bottom of the screen. There was more.

He scrolled down to see a picture of him and Caitlin standing at the eagle habitat talking to the marshal. Another picture followed of them driving off in his mom's minivan.

Then came the words, "Keep quiet or you're next!"

CHAPTER SIX

S am read the message again: Keep quiet or you're
next.

His heart felt like it might beat out of his chest.
This couldn't be happening! He leapt out of his bed
and raced across the hall to Derek's room. "Wake up!"
he whispered harshly, giving Derek a rough shake.

Derek groaned, slowly opening his eyes. "What?"
He looked up at Sam. "What's the matter?"

"You have to see this!" Sam waved the phone in
front of Derek's face.

"Sam, it's the middle of the night..." He rolled over
in his bed. "Come back in the morning."

Sam shook Derek's shoulders again, pulling the
covers off. "No, you have to wake up. I got another
message!"

Derek propped himself up on his elbow and glared at Sam. "What message?"

Sam held up the phone.

Derek's eyebrows raised in the glow. "It works?"

Sam nodded.

The news seemed to perk Derek up. He took the phone and read the screen. "It just says the same thing as before..." He scrolled down. "Oh, man..."

"We have to tell Mom and Dad. Now."

Derek shook his head. "Wait a minute. Let's think about this. If this message is from the bad guys that were chasing the marshal...and he's dead...then they must know you have his phone. They must have seen us with it. Now they're sending you a message, and they have your picture. Maybe they really could come after us. If they know our car, they might know where we live."

Sam hadn't thought about that. He'd assumed telling Mom and Dad would help things, but maybe Derek was right, maybe it would be even more dangerous. Just like those movies where someone is kidnapped and the kidnappers say that if you tell the police the person is dead. He sat down on the floor next to Derek's bed and tried to think. This was very, very bad.

"Maybe we can leave an anonymous tip with the FBI," he said, finally.

Derek dropped his legs over the side of his bed and yawned. "What are you going to tell them? That we saw the marshal, he crashed into you, and then you stole his phone?"

"I didn't steal it. I found it."

"Tell that to the FBI," said Derek. "Maybe you're already on the suspect list."

Sam scratched his head. It was hard to think when he was so tired. "Maybe they could trace the call to see who sent the message."

Derek lay down in his bed. "Maybe we could be dead. Let's go back to sleep and think about it in the morning."

Sam didn't want to go back to bed. He didn't want to get any more messages, and he certainly didn't want to think about the bad guys knowing where he lived.

"Derek..."

"Good night, Sam." Derek put the pillow over his head.

There was nothing else to do but walk back to his room. Sam put the phone in the drawer of his nightstand then lay in his bed, staring at the ceiling for what seemed like forever.

When the sunlight streamed through the window the next morning, Sam felt like he hadn't slept a wink. He reached into his nightstand drawer and picked up the phone. The screen was blank. It was dead. Maybe it had all been just a dream.

He rolled out of bed, got dressed, and walked down to the kitchen. As he ate his cereal, he tried to think about the situation from every direction he could imagine, but he was stumped. He didn't want to tell Mom and Dad if that would put them all in danger. The message said to stay quiet, and maybe that was the best thing to do. But if doing nothing meant something bad was going to happen, how could that be the best thing?

Derek walked in, got his own bowl of cereal, and sat down next to Sam. "Morning."

Sam glared at him. "Is that all you can say?" He usually felt cranky in the morning, but after lying awake half the night, he felt worse than usual.

"No," mumbled Derek between big bites of cereal, "I have a lot more to say."

Sam waited, but his brother just munched on his cereal. "Well?"

"Well, what?"

"What more do you have to say?"

Derek grinned. "I have a plan."

Sam raised his eyebrows. "You do?"

"Yep, but you're not going to like it."

Sam frowned. That wasn't very unusual. He didn't like most of Derek's plans. They normally got them into trouble, or were scary, or dangerous, or all three at once. He took a deep breath. "What's your plan?"

Derek placed his bowl in the sink, then turned his chair around and leaned over the back. "We need to go to Swannanoa."

Sam jumped up from the table. "What? Are you crazy? After the message we got last night? That's the last thing we need to do." He shook his head. "It's way too dangerous."

Derek raised his hand up. "The message said keep quiet, and we're going to. We're not going to tell anyone. But it didn't say don't *do* anything."

Sam scowled at Derek's crazy plan. "We don't even know if this has anything to do with Swannanoa. The message just said the Dooley mansion. It could be Maymont, remember?"

"I thought about that too," said Derek. "But it can't be Maymont. The eagles were stolen from there. The bad guys wouldn't bring the eagles back to the place they just stole them from. That doesn't make any sense."

"*You* don't make any sense," muttered Sam.

"They're going to have to sell them somewhere," Derek continued, ignoring Sam's insult. "What better place than a deserted old mansion in the mountains."

Sam thought about what he said. "You're right."

"I am?"

Sam nodded. "Yep, you're absolutely right. So let's tell the police, and *they* can go to Swannanoa and take care of the whole thing. It'll be great. I'll watch it all on the news right here from the couch."

Derek shook his head. "What fun would that be, Sam?"

Sam's eyes felt like they were bulging out of his head. "Fun? What fun would it be if—" Before he could finish, the phone rang.

Derek looked at the caller ID and handed it to Sam. "Your girlfriend again. Seriously, why don't you just get it over with and tell her you like her."

Sam frowned and yelled into the phone without thinking. "Hello?"

"Sam?"

"Yeah, what is it?"

"Are you all right?" said Caitlin.

"Oh, sure, I'm just great. What can I do for you?" He really wasn't in the mood to talk.

"I've been thinking about the eagles and the 'keep quiet' message."

There was only one way she could know about that —Derek must have called her and told her. Sam sighed into the phone and shot another dirty look at his brother. "You have, huh? Well that seems to be very popular this morning."

"Yes. And I have a plan."

Sam rolled his eyes. "I've had just about enough plans for one morning, Caitlin."

"No, listen," continued Caitlin. "We have to go to Swannanoa."

Sam closed his eyes. This was out of control.

CHAPTER SEVEN

A few days later, Sam was pressing his cheek against the window in the back seat of Mr. Murphy's SUV and watching the river cut its way alongside the twisty mountain road. He felt sick from all the twists and turns, not to mention the reason they were driving up into the mountains.

Caitlin had convinced her dad to drive them past Charlottesville to Afton Mountain for the day. She'd told him there would be some great photo ops on the Blue Ridge Parkway. Since Mr. Murphy was a professional photographer, it was an offer he couldn't turn down. He probably never suspected that the actual reason Caitlin wanted to go was so they could get to Swannanoa on August tenth because of a text message from possible killers, or at the very least professional eagle thieves. No way would Mr. Murphy have said yes to that. Sam was pretty sure *nobody* would have said yes to that. He wasn't sure that eagle thief could really be a profession, but he didn't want to poke around to find out. Anyone low enough to steal bald eagles was not the kind of person Sam wanted to be anywhere near.

He'd tried to protest going on the trip, but it hadn't worked. Derek actually tried to convince Sam that going to Swannanoa was the safest way to figure things out. That seemed crazy, but yet, here he was, sitting in the car driving to Afton Mountain. Derek had said not to worry about it and to live a little. That's exactly what Sam wanted to do—live a little. Going up the mountain toward the killers seemed to be the opposite of that.

"Have you two ever hiked on the Appalachian Trail?" Mr. Murphy asked from the front seat. He wouldn't be so cheerful if he knew the whole point of this trip was to track down killers.

"I don't think so," said Sam flatly.

Caitlin turned around from the front passenger seat. "It's cool. Daddy and I hiked it last year a little bit. Did you know it goes all the way from Georgia to Maine?"

"That's a long hike," said Derek, sitting next to Sam in the back seat.

Caitlin giggled. "We didn't do the whole thing, just

a few miles. We're lucky that it runs through Virginia at all."

Sam remembered hearing a little bit about the trail from his dad. He'd hiked some of the northern parts as a teenager growing up in New York State.

"It's over two thousand miles long," added Mr. Murphy.

Derek whistled. "How much are we going to see today?"

Caitlin held up a map. "Well, I think if we start right here..." she placed her finger on a spot and winked at the boys in the back, "...this would be a good route. Is that okay, Daddy?"

Mr. Murphy nodded. "Sounds good to me. I don't think I've photographed that part of the mountain before." He glanced back in the rearview mirror. "Are you boys up to it?"

"Absolutely," replied Derek. He gave Caitlin a high-five over the headrest of her seat.

"Sure," muttered Sam. He'd resigned himself to the fact they were going, but he was still nervous about it. The place that Caitlin had picked on the map was just a mile from Swannanoa. She and Derek had planned it all out. "Can't wait."

Having Mr. Murphy along on their trip to Swannanoa made Sam feel better, but only a little. After all, if a federal marshal couldn't handle things, Mr. Murphy wouldn't do much better with his camera. Not unless it was one of those James Bond spy cameras that was secretly a scope for a gun. He glanced up at Mr. Murphy in the driver's seat and decided that wasn't very likely. He was a nice guy, but didn't seem the double-oh-seven type.

The drive into the mountains took a little over an hour, and the views out the window showed that they were constantly going up into higher elevation. Some parts next to the road seemed to go straight down. There were guardrails on most of the curves, but some sections of the road had nothing. Sam gulped, thinking about what would happen if a deer ran out in front of the car and they had to swerve. It would be like one last ride at the amusement park with a very bad ending. He sat back and closed his eyes. He was feeling sick to his stomach again. They'd gotten a late start, and it was going to be mid-afternoon before they had lunch on the trail.

Mr. Murphy pulled off into a small parking lot. "What are we doing?" asked Derek. "Is this the trail?"

"It's an overlook," said Caitlin. "A place for travelers to stop and take in the view."

"I'm going to set up my tripod and take some pictures," explained Mr. Murphy. "You guys can look around, but don't get too close to the edge."

Derek hopped out of the car and whistled. "Whoa, check it out!"

They all stepped up to the low, wooden railing at the back of the parking lot. Sam stared out over the edge. He could see for miles down into the valley. The landscape was scattered with fields and farms, wooded sections, buildings, and roads. It reminded him of a model railroad that he'd seen in a museum. Everything looked miniature, like he was looking down from an airplane. It was incredible.

He turned and looked at the roadside marker sign. "What's Rockfish Gap?" he asked.

"It's here," said Caitlin.

Sam frowned at her. "I know it's here. But what is it?"

Mr. Murphy overheard them and laughed. "It's a wind gap, Sam."

"Wind gap?"

"I've heard of those," added Caitlin.

Of course she has, thought Sam.

"It's a gap in the mountain range that was formed by water cutting through, right Daddy?"

Derek looked around. "I don't see any water."

"There's not any water these days," said Mr. Murphy, "but over the centuries there was. Today it's a break in the range, and people have used it as a place to cut through the mountains. Wind gaps are usually where they've built roads, railways, that sort of thing."

Sam looked at the tall mountains on both sides of the valley. Where they were standing didn't seem like something that could be formed by water. Then again, the Grand Canyon didn't seem like it could be formed by water either, but according to his science teacher, it was. Nature was crazy.

No, *he* was crazy. Why was he standing here thinking about nature when there could be danger up ahead? But there was nothing he could do about it right now, was there? Better to push that aside for a few minutes and listen to Mr. Murphy. He was going on about the Blue Ridge Mountains that lay spread out in front of them.

"If you look at them in the right light, the mountains and the trees do have a slight blue tint to them, don't you think?"

Sam stared out at the mountains. They didn't look overly blue to him right then, but he assumed Mr. Murphy knew what he was talking about. Caitlin must get her smarts from somewhere.

While Mr. Murphy set up his camera, Derek called Sam and Caitlin over to the side of the overlook. "I think Swannanoa is up there." He pointed across the road and further up the mountain.

Sam peered up into the trees, holding his hand over his eyes to block the sunshine. "How far?"

Caitlin studied the map. "It looks like the Appalachian trail runs just below us here on the valley side. This road is the Blue Ridge Parkway. The mansion isn't more than a mile north." She pointed up the hill across the road.

"And what exactly do you think is going to happen when we get there?" Sam asked, doing a poor job of holding back his skepticism. "Are they going to throw us a welcome party, hand over the eagles, and send us home?"

Derek shot him an angry glance. "Lighten up, Sam. Geez. You're such a buzz kill. I've been thinking about this. Maybe the killers won't be there yet. Maybe they just stashed the animals there. It's not anywhere close to midnight yet."

Sam closed his eyes. "Oh, that makes me feel much better."

"We'll park the car, hike along the Appalachian Trail for a while, have lunch, then head up to Swannanoa."

"And you think Mr. Murphy will just let us walk right up to an old abandoned building?"

Caitlin raised her palm. "I'll handle that. My dad can't resist a good scene for a photograph. If I tell him there's a secret abandoned mansion for him to shoot at sunset, he'll come with us. Trust me."

Sam wasn't so sure. "But what about the eagles? How are we supposed to save them once we get there?"

"We'll just scout it out," said Derek. "If we find them, we'll call the police, and then we'll be heroes. Just like when I found the lost coins in the cave. Remember how we had our pictures in the paper?"

Sam groaned. Derek had found valuable coins in an old abandoned mine cave in the woods, but he'd also been trapped and almost died.

"Quiet! Here comes my dad," whispered Caitlin.

"Okay, who's ready to pick up some sandwiches and head out on the trail?" asked Mr. Murphy, folding his camera stand.

"Let's do it!" exclaimed Caitlin and Derek.

Sam's stomach growled at the mention of food.

Mr. Murphy looked at him curiously. "Sam, you okay?"

"Yeah, just still a little car sick." Those twists and turns on the road *had* left him feeling a bit off, and while a snack did sound good, it wasn't the main reason he felt queasy. He glanced back up the mountain, picturing Swannanoa behind the thick tree line. He wondered if the eagles really were up there, and if they were, what else might be there with them.

Just down the road was a group of buildings that

seemed to be part convenience store, part gas station, and part tourist center. Several other structures around the corner were run down and closed off, and a motel sat up on the hill above the roadway.

"Let's get some food for lunch on the trail," said Mr. Murphy, turning into the parking lot. "You guys go ahead and I'll fill up the car with gas."

After a bathroom break and a few minutes of shopping, Sam followed Caitlin out of the store. He held a bag with two bottles of water in one hand, and a bag of chips and a sandwich in the other. Derek strutted out behind them wearing a pair of goofy reflective sunglasses.

"Where did you get those?" asked Sam.

"I bought them," said Derek, peeking over the top of the shiny lenses. "I'm undercover..." he glanced back and forth, then lowered his voice to a whisper, "for our secret mission."

Sam shook his head. "They might be a little dark for the trail."

Derek pushed the shades back in place and grinned like he was on the cover of a magazine. "Admit it, they look good."

Caitlin turned around and giggled. "You're something else, Derek."

Derek flashed a cocky smile. "That's what everyone keeps saying..."

They walked over to where Mr. Murphy was still filling up the car with gas. "I got your lunch, Daddy," said Caitlin, holding up a bag.

Before Mr. Murphy could reply, a loud rumbling sound echoed through the valley, growing into a roar as a group of motorcycles rolled around the corner and turned into the parking lot.

Mr. Murphy eyed the line of bikers suspiciously. "Why don't you get in the car, guys. I'm almost done filling up."

Sam looked over at the group of bikers. There had to be more than a dozen of them. He looked at the jacket of one of the bikers and saw something familiar.

"Where are you going?" called Caitlin to Derek who was already halfway across the parking lot, walking toward the bikers.

"Derek!" said Mr. Murphy, tightening the gas cap. "It's time to go."

But Derek didn't stop. He walked right up to the closest biker and waved. Sam couldn't see the biker's face, but he wondered what the guy must think of his nutty brother wearing those stupid-looking sunglasses. He had to give it to him though, Derek certainly wasn't afraid of making a fool of himself.

Sam was too far away to hear what Derek was saying to the biker, but suddenly the man let out a big laugh and gave Derek a high five. That laugh sounded familiar too. Derek turned and waved at Sam and Caitlin to come over.

"You know who that must be, don't you?" said Caitlin.

Sam had put it together right about the same time she did. "The Confederate Ghosts?"

Caitlin nodded. "I think so. It's okay, Daddy, they're friendly."

Mr. Murphy watched cautiously as Sam and Caitlin joined Derek next to the bikes. Sam stared at the shiny chrome reflecting the sunlight. The black and silver Harleys seemed a little big for him, although he remembered riding on the back of one leaving Belle Isle once before.

"Guys, look, it's Mad Dog, from the Ghosts!" exclaimed Derek. "You remember him, don't you?"

Mad Dog turned off the engine and stepped off the motorcycle, straightening to his full height. Sam had forgotten how tall the man was. He must be at least six foot four. Sam waved weakly and tried to smile. "Hey."

"Hi," said Caitlin.

"How about that, running into you kids up here." Mad Dog chuckled in his deep, gravelly voice. "We're fixin' to put up over there at the motel around the bend." He pointed to the building higher up on the side of the mountain. He set his helmet down on the seat of his bike and wiped his forehead.

Luke 'Mad Dog' DeWitt was the leader of the Confederate Ghosts, a biker gang from Richmond. Sam had been scared to death when they'd run into him at Hollywood Cemetery last summer, and then again when they found their hideout at night on Belle Isle, but his bark turned out to be worse than his bite. He was a really nice guy.

"What are you doing up here?" Sam was starting to feel a little more comfortable talking to the biker again.

"Riding, of course." Mad Dog swept one arm out behind him. "Look around! Have you ever seen a more gorgeous place?"

"It's beautiful," said Caitlin.

"Like a little slice of heaven up here in God's creation," said Mad Dog. "Trust me kids, you haven't lived until you've felt the wind in your face under a sunshine-dripped day up on top of the mountain. It's magic."

Sam nodded. He stared up at the sunny blue sky and imagined touring around the curvy mountain roads without a roof over his head. As dangerous as Mom always said riding a motorcycle was, it did seem pretty fun on a summer day.

Mr. Murphy walked up behind them. "Ready to go, kids?" He eyed Mad Dog and the motorcycles cautiously.

"Yeah, let's ride!" proclaimed Derek, acting like he was going to jump onto one of the bikes.

"Easy there, partner," Mad Dog chuckled. "You might need a few more gallons in your tank before you're ready to ride the great blue yonder with us."

Derek frowned. "I was afraid you'd say that."

Mr. Murphy agreed. "Let's stick to the car today, guys." He stuck his arm out and shook hands with Mad Dog. "Nice to meet you."

"You've got a good group of kids here, friend. What brings the four of you up this way?"

Mr. Murphy pointed down the slope to the other side of the road. "A little hiking, maybe taking some photographs."

"Right on, man," said Mad Dog. "Sounds like a fun time." He turned back to Derek. "Well, y'all have a good time. Enjoy this weather."

"All right, see ya," said Sam, already backpedaling toward the car. It was cool to see the bikers again, but they'd made him nervous enough the first time they met. As fun as it looked, one motorcycle ride had been enough for him.

"Nice to see you," said Caitlin. "Say hi to the others for us."

"I'll do that," waved Mad Dog, strapping on his helmet and slinging a leg over his bike. He stomped his foot down on a pedal near the ground and the engine roared to life. "See you out on the road!"

When they got back into the car, Mr. Murphy glanced over at the group of bikers with a puzzled expression. "Tell me again how you know those guys?"

"It's a long story, Daddy," Caitlin giggled. She looked back at Sam and winked. "I'll tell you out on the trail."

CHAPTER EIGHT

M r. Murphy drove down the road to a parking spot marked for Appalachian Trail hikers. They put their food and drink into the school-sized backpacks that they'd brought with them. Sam took a canteen filled with water out of his pack and attached it to his belt. Mr. Murphy had a larger backpack with lots of pockets and zippers to hold his camera equipment and tripod.

"Is that all camera equipment in your pack?" asked Sam. "It looks heavy." He knew Mr. Murphy was a professional photographer but was impressed at how well he looked the part.

Mr. Murphy smiled. "Mostly camera gear, but some hiking and emergency packets too. It's good to be prepared when you're out in the wild in a place like the Appalachian Trail."

"Emergency?" Derek's ears perked up. "What kind of emergency packets? Do you have a Taser?"

Sam shook his head. "Why would we need a Taser?"

"I don't know, Sam, in case we needed to *Tase someone...*" He drilled a hard stare at Sam. It took a minute for Sam to realize that Derek was talking about running into bad guys at Swannanoa.

"No Tasers, sorry, Derek," chuckled Mr. Murphy. "But I do have a first aid kit, a compass, and a whistle."

"A whistle?" asked Caitlin. "What do we need that for?"

Mr. Murphy pulled out a flat, orange, plastic whistle attached to a cord that could hook to a back-pack. "In case we get lost, it lets off a shrill sound that can be heard a long distance."

"Can I try?" asked Derek.

"Sure," said Mr. Murphy, handing the whistle to Derek. "Just once, though, and don't blow too hard. We don't want any other hikers out here to think that we have an emergency."

"It's not that loud, is it, Daddy?" asked Caitlin.

"The package said it's one hundred and twenty decibels, which is about as loud as a rock concert."

"Wow," said Caitlin.

Sam noticed his brother's devilish grin as he put the

whistle to his lips. "Not too hard, Derek. Don't burst our eardrums."

Derek blew into the whistle. Sam covered his ears. It sounded like a teapot was exploding right next to him. It was so loud!

"Whoa," said Derek, handing it back to Mr. Murphy. "That's cool."

"It's just for emergencies. I don't expect we'll have to use it, but it's always good to be prepared."

Caitlin nodded. "Daddy hiked a whole part of the trail when he was in college, didn't you?"

"I did. And I learned the hard way that you need to be prepared."

"Why, what happened?" asked Sam.

"My buddies and I were up in Maine, near the end of a week-long hike. We'd forgotten to read the forecast at the last checkpoint. A storm rolled in during the night, and we had to hustle down off the mountain before there was a mudslide. We nearly got stuck up there."

"Wow," said Sam, glancing over his shoulder at the car. He was glad they wouldn't be hiking too far today.

"All right," said Mr. Murphy, pulling on his pack and tightening the straps. "Let's get going."

They walked to the edge of the parking lot where a small trail cut through high grass and into a wooded area. "Caitlin, you're our navigator today," said Mr. Murphy. "Which way should we go?"

Caitlin held up a trail map she'd bought at the convenience store. It showed more detail of this part of the Appalachian Trail and surrounding trails than the larger Virginia highway map she'd had in the car. "Let's head south for a couple miles and then..." she moved her finger along the dotted lines on the paper, "then we can loop up above the highway on this other trail for a bit. It should get us back pretty close to where we parked." She looked up and winked at Derek.

"Sounds good," said Derek with a quick nod.

Sam rolled his eyes. Enough with the winking. It was like they were communicating in code. He wasn't so crazy about the two of them devising the whole plan without him. He wasn't exactly jealous, but he did feel a little left out. How did he always get himself into messes like this?

"All right, then, let's head out," said Mr. Murphy.

"Onward and upward!" yelled Derek.

Caitlin tapped Sam's shoulder and smiled. "Aren't you excited? This is going to be fun."

Sam tried to fake a happy face. "Uh huh."

Caitlin shook her head. "Come on. It's an adventure. Try to relax."

Sam was skeptical. He wondered if she was getting a little too excited about going on adventures and solving mysteries. "You're starting to sound like Derek more and more every minute."

Caitlin dropped her jaw playfully. "I'm highly offended." She stepped up behind her dad and Derek. "Come on!"

* * *

THE AIR WAS COOL up on the mountain, despite it being a sunny, August, Virginia day, and it felt good to be walking outside. Sam guessed the elevation helped keep things from getting as hot as it did back home. The trail cut in and out of the trees, adding pockets of shade from the sun. Mr. Murphy said the patches of paint on the trees were white blazes that marked the Appalachian Trail. In some places it was straight, in other places it wound around stones, roots, and trees and up and down ridges and valleys. It was sweet.

After they'd hiked a while, Mr. Murphy stopped at a clearing with a direct view of the Rockfish Valley. He pulled out his camera, snapping shots from different angles and directions. Derek stood and watched him operate his camera equipment while Sam and Caitlin kept walking further down the trail.

"Did you hear what Billy did to Mr. Clancy on the last week of school?" said Caitlin.

Sam shook his head, knowing that she was going to

tell him no matter what he said. Caitlin seemed to have been talking non-stop since they'd headed out on their hike. He wondered if that was why Mr. Murphy had let them keep walking after he had stopped. It would be tough to get many pictures of wildlife with her making so much noise.

He looked back at Derek behind them. Mr. Murphy seemed to be giving him some lessons about how to use the camera.

"Can you believe it?" said Caitlin.

Sam looked back at her. He hadn't been listening. "What?"

Caitlin frowned but kept on talking. "I said, Billy took all of the staples out of his stapler and all the pencils from his desk."

Sam lowered his eyebrows, trying to figure out what he'd missed. "Whose desk?"

"Mr. Clancy's!" She dropped her jaw open again like it was the most shocking thing in the world. "Can you believe it? Isn't that so mean?"

Sam nodded. There wasn't much that their friend Billy Maxwell could do that would surprise him, but he wasn't in the mood to think about school right then. He was still feeling nervous about going to Swannanoa. His stomach rumbled, reminding him of the sandwich in his backpack. The only thing he wanted to think about right now was lunch. The afternoon was getting late, and he still hadn't eaten. Things always seemed more stressful when he was hungry.

Caitlin glanced over and giggled. She must have heard his stomach.

"There's a nice flat rock," she said. "Why don't we stop and eat?"

Sam sighed in relief. "That's a great idea."

They sat down and gazed across the valley, the fields and houses still seeming a million miles away from where they were up on the trail. Derek and Mr. Murphy walked past, saying they were going to continue a few more minutes up the trail to let Derek keep experimenting with the camera.

Sam opened his pack, pulling out his sandwich, chips, and drink. He poured the water into the now empty canteen he had attached to his belt.

"Who do you think you're going to get for a teacher this year?" asked Caitlin.

Sam took a bite of his sandwich, already feeling better for sitting down. "I don't know," he answered with his mouth full. "I think Ms. Allen. Derek had her and said she was cool. She let them watch a lot of—" He stopped mid-sentence, eyeing the bushes on the edge of the trail behind Caitlin. They were shaking.

"Movies?" said Caitlin, finishing his sentence. "I know. Becky's sister told her the same thing. I don't know how they get through their work for the year with all those movies." She took a breath and looked up at Sam. He was frozen, sandwich hanging in mid-air, staring at the bushes. "What's wrong?"

The branches stopped shaking. Then something walked onto the trail. A huge something.

A black bear.

CHAPTER NINE

"Don't move..." Sam whispered, barely loud enough to hear. He didn't want to startle the bear.

"What is it?" Caitlin turned her head and then put her hand over her mouth to stifle a squeal. "Oh my gosh!"

They both sat frozen like statues, watching the bear lumber across the grassy trail. Sam couldn't tell if it had noticed them, but he slowly lowered his sandwich to his lap. Maybe the bear had smelled their lunches.

"What do we do?" whispered Caitlin.

"I don't know. Can you see your dad?"

Caitlin inched her head to the side for a glimpse further up the trail. "I don't see him," she whispered back.

The bear was fifty feet from where they sat. It

seemed to be smelling the air. Sam couldn't believe how big it was. Sure, he'd seen bears on TV and in the zoo. He'd even seen one just the other day at Maymont, but there had always been a fence standing between them. There was no fence here on the trail, just grass and air. He remembered Mr. Haskins mentioning that bears and snakes lived up in the mountains, but he'd been too focused on the eagles to really think about it much. Well, he was thinking about it now.

The bear's fur was dark black and looked thick. Its long nose had a touch of brown near the end, like a German Shepherd. A memory flashed through Sam's mind of the time he and Derek had been exploring the woods behind their house. They'd thought they'd seen a bear, but it had only turned out to be someone's pet dog. There was no confusion this time. This was definitely a bear.

Sam nervously shifted his weight, but the canteen on his belt bumped his backpack, which tumbled over on the rock. The bear turned toward the noise, eyes staring right at them. Then it reared up on its hind legs, its nose sniffing the air. Sam thought his heart was going to bust right out of his chest.

"I think we need to get out of here," whispered Caitlin.

"No, we don't want it to chase us."

The bear lowered back to the ground and began moving toward them.

"Sam!" Caitlin cried.

His mind raced. What should they do? He looked behind them, but the mountain fell away in a steep grade that would be too hard to climb down. They were trapped.

The bear moved closer. There was no choice. They had to move now!

Sam carefully stood on the rock, motioning for Caitlin to do the same. "Nice and easy."

He grabbed for what he could of his scattered stuff, throwing the remaining food over the bear's head. It didn't move as they stepped off the rock and began inching slowly up the trail. Sam hurled the metal canteen into the bushes as far away from them as possible. For a moment the bear seemed distracted, but then it turned and started toward them again.

As Sam crept backward, his foot caught on a tree root and he slipped to the ground.

"Sam!" Caitlin bent over and grabbed his arm.

He tried to yell for help, but his mouth was dry as he stared into the bear's eyes. Visions of being mauled by the beast flashed through his head. It seemed to be looking right at him.

Just as he was sure he was a goner, a shrill whistle sounded from behind them on the trail. "Hey!" a deep voice yelled, followed by clapping hands, then a whistle again.

They turned around and saw Derek and Mr. Murphy moving slowly toward them. Mr. Murphy had the emergency whistle in his mouth and blew it again. "Walk toward us, slowly," he ordered.

Sam scrambled to his feet and backed up along the trail with Caitlin until they reached Mr. Murphy and Derek.

"Stay here," Mr. Murphy said firmly.

Derek's eyes were wild with excitement as he held up the camera, snapping pictures of the bear. Sam wondered again about Mr. Murphy's camera being a James Bond spy camera with a gun inside. Even if it was, Derek would be more likely to take a selfie with the bear than do something useful to save them.

Mr. Murphy took three steps toward the bear. "Go on, get going!" he yelled. He held his hands up over his head like someone pretending to be a ghost. Sam thought he'd seen that on the Nature Channel as a way to scare bears. He wished he'd thought of that earlier.

The bear stood still, like it was considering what this strange creature was saying. For a moment, Sam worried that it would charge right at Mr. Murphy and devour him, whistle and all. But then, all at once, it turned and lumbered in the opposite direction. It stopped at Sam's sandwich, picked it up in its mouth with one big bite, and then disappeared into the bushes moving south down the side of the mountain.

For a long time, they all just stood there, staring at the place where the bear had entered the bushes. Sam kept thinking that the sandwich could have been his head.

Finally, after it seemed sure that the bear wasn't coming back, Mr. Murphy turned around and walked over to them. He put his arms around Caitlin and hugged her. "You guys okay?"

Sam nodded slowly.

"That was awesome!" exclaimed Derek. "The guys are not going to believe that I saw a bear. One on one, in the middle of the trail. It was him or me, and he blinked first."

"Is he gone?" asked Caitlin. Sam thought he saw a tear in her eye.

"I think so." Mr. Murphy hugged her tight. "You're okay. That was quite an encounter."

Sam finally exhaled. He'd been holding his breath without realizing it. He turned to his brother and snapped out of his trance. "One on one? There are four of us here, Derek."

Derek laughed, holding up the camera. "Yeah, well I have the pictures to prove it."

"Maybe we should just skip looking for Swan-nanoa," Caitlin said to Derek when they were out of earshot from her dad. Her voice sounded shaky, which was understandable. They were both rattled by the encounter with the bear. Sam had felt pretty rattled even *before* the bear.

"Finally!" Sam threw his hands in the air. "That's the smartest thing you've said all day."

Caitlin frowned, but kept talking to Derek. "I mean, maybe Sam's right, maybe this really is too dangerous."

Before Derek could answer, the sharp cry of a bird pierced the sky overhead. They all looked up to see huge wings circling in the clear blue sky.

Sam could just make out the unmistakable white feathers on its head. "Wow, it's a bald eagle." Could it be one of the Maymont eagles? No, the thieves wouldn't let them fly free like that. They'd have them in cages somewhere. These were wild eagles. But still, it seemed like a sign.

"Save the eagles," said Derek. "They need us."

They stood, watching the majestic bird circle above them. Mr. Murphy stepped up slowly behind them, the shutter on his camera whirring quietly.

Caitlin's face turned serious. She looked over at Sam. "Derek's right."

Sam shook his head. "Caitlin..."

But she kept talking. "They *do* need us. And we have to try to save them."

"Who needs you?" asked Mr. Murphy.

"The eagles, Daddy. They have to be protected. We can't let them go extinct." She turned back and smiled sheepishly at the boys.

Mr. Murphy nodded. "You're right, sweetie. We owe it to them to live responsibly and take care of the planet."

Sam put his hand over his eyes and shook his head. He'd come so close to convincing them to leave.

Caitlin's enthusiasm for the mission quickly bounced back as if she'd never even seen the bear. She pulled the map out of her backpack. "I was looking at the map, Daddy, and this is the other trail I was talking about." She pointed toward the path that led up the ridge to their right. "It says there's a scenic overlook that is perfect for sunset pictures. You don't want to miss that, do you?"

Her dad's eyes lit up and he glanced at his watch. "I don't know, it's getting late...we don't want to be out here after dark."

Caitlin nodded in agreement. "We won't be. It's only a short walk from there back to our car."

Mr. Murphy thought for a moment, glancing off at the horizon. Then he turned back to Caitlin and the boys. "Okay, but once we get the pictures, we're going straight to the parking lot."

Caitlin smiled. "Perfect. It will be worth it. I promise."

Caitlin's new trail wasn't nearly as wide or as well maintained as the Appalachian Trail. Sam wondered if it was even a trail at all. It seemed more like a spot where the deer, or maybe bears, had worn down a path to get up and down the mountain.

Derek had a pretty good sense of direction, so combined with Caitlin's map, there wasn't too much of a chance that they'd get lost. Of course, neither of those things would do much good if they ran into trouble with the killers, or another bear, but Sam tried not to think about that. He couldn't exactly run home by himself now.

He knew the only reason they were taking this route was to get up to Swannanoa. He was tempted to blurt out the whole crazy plan to Mr. Murphy right then and there, but he held back. As much as he always hated the half-brained plans that Derek came up with, there was still a part of him that hated to be left behind. A small part, but even with the terrifying situations Derek managed to get them into, they did usually end up solving some pretty epic mysteries. And he found some comfort in the fact that Caitlin was on board. She wasn't as reckless as his brother, at least not usually. Leave it to Sam to pick the worst time to listen to her.

After a few minutes of pretty steep climbing, they reached the road, just around the bend from where they'd stopped at the overlook that morning. Caitlin's dad warned them to be careful when they crossed over to the north side of the Blue Ridge Parkway. Even though it was called a Parkway, it was just a two-lane road that cut through the mountains. While it was a main passage for tourists, there wasn't much traffic today.

Mr. Murphy said that in the winter months, parts of the Parkway were closed down due to the snow and icy conditions up on the top of the mountain. He said that in some spots, the highway department even put runway lights, like they use at the airport, on the sides of the roads to keep people from driving over the edge during fog and other bad weather.

Any road that needed those kinds of lights to keep you on it couldn't be a very safe road to begin with, but Sam didn't say anything about that either as they crossed. Before long, the wooded trail began to widen, opening to a clearing and a gravel road.

"Are you sure you know where we're headed, Caitlin?" Mr. Murphy said, eyeing the trees for a trail marker. "This looks like someone's driveway, maybe."

Caitlin smiled and pointed up ahead. "It's just around this corner. We're almost there."

Sam wondered if *his* dad would have gone along with such a reckless plan. Probably not, he decided, and he bet that Derek knew it as well. It was likely part of the reason they'd recruited Mr. Murphy to drive. He seemed a lot more relaxed, taking things as they came. Plus, he was used to trusting Caitlin, so he hadn't grown as suspicious of possible secret plans. Sam wondered how many more adventures Caitlin would have to go on with him and Derek before her parents started being as cautious as Mom and Dad. Not many, he thought, as a white marble railing came into view up ahead.

"Holy cow!" exclaimed Derek.

Sam squinted as the low afternoon sunshine glinted through the branches. A massive building hid behind a row of tall spruce trees past the railings.

Swannanoa.

As they walked closer, Sam could see that it was much bigger than the mansion at Maymont. It had a totally different look, with a light-colored stone exterior and orangish-red roof tiles, reminding him of buildings he'd seen in pictures from his parents' trip to Europe. Most of the structure was two stories high, but as they moved alongside, he saw a pair of rectangular towers on both sides of the front, adding two more floors above the roofline. There were dozens of windows and doors, each with fancy arches, pillars, and engravings built into them. A railed marble patio ran along the front, with a small set of stairs leading down to the grass.

"It really *is* a palace," marveled Caitlin.

"Did you know this was back here?" asked Mr. Murphy, his eyebrows raised in surprise. "Is this where you meant to take us?"

"Um, well…" mumbled Caitlin, nervously tugging on a strand of her long hair.

Sam hadn't seen her at a loss for words very often. Clearly they couldn't keep her dad in the dark forever.

Sam couldn't stand it one more minute. "Something bad might be happening here!"

There. He'd said it.

CHAPTER TEN

After Sam's outburst, a silent pause followed. He glanced at Derek who was shaking his head. Caitlin was looking at her feet.

"Well," said Sam, "somebody had to tell him!"

Mr. Murphy raised his eyebrows even more. "I think you guys need to tell me exactly what's going on. Don't tell me that we just stumbled upon this mansion out here in the woods by accident."

Caitlin let out a long breath and frowned at Sam, although he thought he noticed a hint of relief on her face. She probably didn't like misleading her dad either.

Derek spoke up first. "It's my fault. I convinced them it was a good idea."

Caitlin shook her head. "No, that's not true. It was my idea too."

Mr. Murphy looked confused. "What was your idea?"

"The eagles," said Sam. "The ones that were stolen from Maymont."

"The eagles?"

"We think they're being sold here," explained Caitlin. "Tonight. At midnight." She told him about seeing the man at Maymont, how he had crashed into Sam while being chased by the two other men, how they found his phone and the message, and finally how Sam received the threatening pictures and the warning not to tell anyone.

"So you see, Daddy, we couldn't tell you. We were afraid something would happen."

Mr. Murphy had sat down on an old fallen log. His elbows were perched on his knees and he rested his chin on his hand. He looked like one of those ancient sculptures of someone thinking, which was what he seemed to be doing. For a minute he didn't say anything.

"I'm sorry, Daddy."

"Yeah," said Derek. "I guess we shouldn't have lied to you."

Mr. Murphy raised his head and looked at them. "So despite all this, you really don't know if anything is going on here at all? The message could just as well have been about Maymont?"

They all stared at the ground.

"Maybe," admitted Caitlin.

"But you do know that someone sent you a threatening message. Which you should have turned into the police, or at the very least your parents."

"Or the FBI," added Sam.

Caitlin shushed him to be quiet. "I guess you're right."

"By rushing off on this secret trip without telling me the truth, you might have put us all in more danger instead of less." He stood up, staring toward Swannanoa. "I think you've let your imaginations get the best of you with this old place. It looks pretty abandoned to me."

He pulled out his cell phone and grimaced. "No service."

"So what should we do now?" asked Derek.

"Go home," said Sam. "That's what I've been trying to say all along." He didn't want to say I told you so, but he *had* told them so.

Mr. Murphy nodded. "That's a good idea, Sam. I'm sure this is private property. We shouldn't even be up here."

Caitlin held the map up to her face, and then pointed down the hill. "If we follow the driveway, it will take us to the road with the gas station and back to the car in the parking lot."

"Let's go," encouraged Sam, stepping forward. They

walked across the grass to the driveway, pausing in front of the building. There didn't seem to be anyone around at all. No cars, no people. It was just as Mr. Haskins had said the other day. It was abandoned.

Another distant cry from a hawk or an eagle sounded from some high tree out of sight. There was a long view to the valley, the sky showing just a hint of color. The sun was dropping faster, its golden beams streaming over the treetops, reflecting off the red tile roof of the building.

It was as if everyone had the same idea at once, but Caitlin spoke first. "Why don't we just stay for the sunset, Daddy? You could get some amazing pictures up here. We owe that to you. It's the least we can do."

"Yeah, look at these views!" Derek shouted.

Mr. Murphy looked over at him. "Sam, I know you were anxious to go..."

Sam sighed, hesitant to give in when they were so close to going home, but everyone seemed to have given up the thought of finding the eagles, and it was a beautiful spot. He rolled his eyes and nodded.

"Well," said Mr. Murphy, staring off at the colorful horizon, "Maybe just a few minutes..." He pulled his tripod from his backpack.

"Great," said Caitlin. "I'll help you."

"While you guys take pictures, we're going to walk around," said Derek.

Mr. Murphy gave them a cautious glance.

Derek held up his hand like he was taking an oath. "Not far, honest. We'll stay right around the palace here."

"Stay where I can see you, Derek. I'm serious. It's going to be dark soon, and I don't want to have to come looking for you two." Mr. Murphy pointed to the sky, which by now was bursting with color. "We've had enough adventure for one day, I think."

"Great. Come on, Sam." Derek bounded off, heading toward some old fountains they'd passed.

Sam was tired of exploring, but he didn't want to leave Derek by himself, so he trailed a little distance behind, gazing at the mansion. Tucked behind the tall evergreens, it seemed almost like it was hiding. How many people even knew it was up here? He tried to imagine what it must have been like to live in such a place, set majestically way up on top of a mountain.

He ran and caught up with Derek. "Can you believe that the Dooleys owned this place *and* Maymont?"

"Yeah, quite a summer house, huh?" Derek answered. "What's that over there?" He pointed to another building that was covered in ivy and mostly hidden behind another tall evergreen tree.

"Hey," Sam called out. "We're supposed to stay close enough to see Mr. Murphy."

Derek turned and shaded his eyes with one hand. "I can still see him."

Sam humphed. "Barely."

Derek walked farther from Caitlin and her dad, but Sam stayed put.

"It's a tower!" Derek shouted.

Sam took a few more steps, just to see what Derek was yelling about. The tower was just like you'd see on the corner of a castle or read about in a fairy tale where a princess is locked up in the top or an evil wizard is working on his spells. It had a rounded, sloping roof with the same tiles as the mansion, and several long narrow windows decorated the top all around. It had to be part of Swannanoa. No one would build a tower out in the middle of the woods unless it was part of this place.

The sound of a motor came rumbling up through the trees. "Somebody's coming! Sam, get down!"

Sam sprinted toward Derek and together they crawled behind a rock. They were far beyond Mr. Murphy's view by now, but that seemed less important than the silver pickup that came into view. It rolled to a stop next to a small cottage they hadn't noticed in the woods. It looked like an old caretaker's house or servants' quarters made out of rough stones.

A man stepped out and walked up to the cottage.

Sam couldn't see his face, but noticed he was wearing heavy-duty work gloves.

"What's he doing?" Sam whispered as the man opened the door with a key and went inside.

"I don't know, stay down," said Derek.

A minute later, the man emerged carrying a large wire cage. When he set it down on the ground to open the tailgate of the truck, Sam could see that there was an animal inside. "The eagles!" he almost shouted out.

"Shh!" Derek hissed. "Be quiet or he'll hear us."

The man lifted the large cage, sliding it into the back of the pickup. As he did, he raised his face in plain view of the boys.

Sam gasped. It was one of the men who had been chasing the marshal at Maymont. Sam's heartbeat was pounding in his ears. He'd almost stopped worrying about anything dangerous happening, but now his fears came rushing back.

"I knew it," said Derek. "It's them."

They watched the man go back into the building, returning with two more cages, filled with creatures of different shapes and sizes. When the cages were all in the truck bed, he locked the door to the cottage, pulling a radio from his belt.

"Everything's secured. I'm coming back."

He started up the truck and drove off toward the palace, barely missing where they were hiding. Sam wondered how many men there were. The man in the truck was talking to someone on the radio. The second guy was probably at the palace. Was it just the two of them from Maymont, or were there more?

Sam looked in the direction of the mansion where Caitlin and her dad were taking pictures. He couldn't see them any longer, but the man was headed straight for them. Then he remembered something. "The picture," Sam muttered.

"What picture?"

"The one that they sent to me on the marshal's phone. It was of us. They know who we are. They'll recognize Caitlin! We have to do something!"

CHAPTER ELEVEN

Derek nodded and they scurried along the tree line, moving quickly toward the house but staying out of view. Sam didn't know what he would do, but he couldn't let them just take Caitlin and her dad. He remembered the scared look on the marshal's face in the Japanese Gardens. They hadn't been able to save him, but there was still time to save Caitlin and her dad. They just had to hurry.

They reached the side of the mansion and tried to catch their breaths. Sam crept up to the front of the mansion and peered around the corner. He was relieved when he saw Caitlin and Mr. Murphy standing near the patio. There was still time.

He stepped forward into the yard to wave to Caitlin but stopped short when she looked at him with a cold stare. He backed up cautiously to the edge of the wall, just as a man appeared behind her.

He was holding a gun.

Sam watched from around the corner as the man marched Caitlin and her dad up the stone patio steps and into the mansion, the gun pointed at them menacingly. Sam inched backwards, his shoulders pressed against the marble of the building, then slid down into the grass.

"Oh my gosh." He started to feel dizzy.

Derek came behind him and stared around the corner. "Sam, calm down. Getting hysterical isn't going to help anything. We have to think."

"Think?" Sam moaned. "How can I think? You know what happened to the marshal? They killed him. What do you think they'll do to a girl and a photographer if they killed a federal marshal?" He put his head in his hands. "We should never have come up here. What were we thinking?"

Derek paced around, staring up at the building. The brilliant orange in the sky was already beginning to fade. "It's getting dark, but the message said that the buyers aren't coming until midnight, so we should have some time."

"Time?" Sam raised his head. "Time for what? How can we possibly do anything? They have guns."

"I have a plan," Derek said, confidently.

"No way. No more of your plans. That's what got us in this mess."

"Well what do you want to do, Sam?" Derek hissed. "We can't just sit here and cry. We have to try to save them."

Sam shot an angry stare at his brother. "This is all your fault. I told you we shouldn't have come!"

Derek bent down and looked Sam in the eyes. "Do *you* have a plan?"

Sam thought about it for a moment then wearily shook his head. He really didn't know what to do.

"Okay then, listen to me," said Derek. "I need you to stay here. I'm going to run down to the road and find some help. That's the only way."

Sam looked up at his insane brother. "You want me to stay here alone? Are you kidding?"

"If we both leave, those men could take Caitlin and Mr. Murphy somewhere else and we wouldn't even know it. One of us has to keep watch, and one of us has to go and get help. Remember that store we stopped at down the road? Would you rather go?"

Sam forced himself to think it through. It made sense for Derek to go. He was a faster runner, and he had a good sense of direction. Sam didn't trust himself to find the store they'd stopped at earlier. He'd probably end up wandering lost through the woods, and that wouldn't help them at all.

"No, you go. I'll stay here."

Derek nodded. "Just stay hidden and you'll be fine. I'll be back in no time. It's not that far."

"Yeah, if you can find it in the dark."

"I'll find it," said Derek. "Don't worry. Just keep watch, okay?"

Once again, Sam didn't like the plan, but he couldn't think of anything better. "Okay, but hurry." He stood up and gave his brother a good luck pat on the shoulder. "And Derek?" he said, as his brother began to walk away.

Derek stopped and looked back. "Yeah?"

"Be careful."

Derek nodded, then bolted for the trees. Sam watched him run along the edge of the grassy yard to the driveway that led down the mountaintop toward the road.

Sam wondered how his brother could be so brave. Sure he was goofy and annoying most of the time, but he always seemed to pull it together when things got tough. Sam hoped Derek would be all right. He hoped they'd all be all right.

When Derek was out of view, Sam stood up and looked for a better hiding spot. He spied a clump of overgrown bushes along the house, and began slinking quickly toward them. He was halfway there when headlights came up ahead of him from the driveway. He dropped to the ground.

For a split second, he hoped it was Derek bringing help, but he knew there hadn't been enough time for that. He crawled cautiously through the grass toward the mansion to get a better view. It was the pickup, pulling to a stop near the front door.

The man from the tower stepped out of the truck and was greeted by the man with the gun. Sam shuddered, clearly remembering them both from Maymont. It was the two killers. He listened carefully to what they were saying from his hiding spot in the grass.

"I just heard from the buyers," said the gun man. "They're moving things up from midnight."

Sam gulped at the news. He thought back to the message on the phone about the buyers coming to the Dooley mansion at midnight. By now, there was no question they were at the right mansion, but they might not have as much time as they thought. The deal could be happening any minute!

He looked back down the driveway, hoping to see Derek appearing with help, but it was like he'd been swallowed up in the darkness. Could he get help in time?

"Moving up? Till when?" the man from the truck asked, his hands on his hips.

"Dunno. But we need to be ready."

The truck man nodded with a grunt. "Good. The sooner we can get these things out of here the better. I don't like the heat that's coming down on us, Dex."

"Also, we had some unexpected visitors," said the man named Dex. "But don't worry about them, they're secured upstairs." He turned and pointed up at the mansion. "One of those kids from Maymont and her dad."

The other man shook his head and began pacing nervously in the driveway. "What are they doing here? You said this was going to be easy, Dex!"

"Hey, let's just get this deal done. Then we won't have to worry about anything else except counting the waves on the beach." He patted the other man on the back.

"I don't like this, Dex. I still have some animals out in the cottage. If they're coming earlier, we need to hustle and get them all over here."

"Better get going, then."

"I'm not doing it by myself, man. Come on, give me a hand."

As Sam listened in the grass, he felt something moving beside him. He glanced back at his legs. A snake was slithering toward him! He gasped, jumping to his feet, and ran behind the corner of the palace.

"What was that?" he heard one man say.

"Go check it out. Then meet me by the tower," Dex answered. "And Cody?"

"Yeah?"

"I don't need any more surprises." The pickup door slammed and Dex drove off.

Sam's eyes opened wide, still looking for the snake, but also now hearing the footsteps of the man named Cody as he moved toward him on the gravel path circling the mansion. Time to hide!

Sam ran along the rear of the building until he saw a recessed side door. He backed into the doorway, his hand shaking as he felt for the knob. A shadow appeared on the ground at the corner of the building. It grew closer and closer as Sam found the handle and pushed the door open. He slipped into the mansion, shutting the door softly behind him. He crouched down against the inside wall, listening to the footsteps crunch right outside the door.

CHAPTER TWELVE

Inside the mansion, Sam pressed himself against the wall as the footsteps walked past the door on the other side. Was the man still there?

Sam counted to fifty and then again to twenty, just to be safe. He inched his nose to the windowsill, peering through the dusty glass. The man seemed to be gone. He was safe for now.

He let out a deep breath and tried to take in his surroundings. Sam guessed that he'd entered a back dining hall or study. The room had high ceilings, decorated with wood trim carved into shapes like honeycomb from a beehive. A wide fireplace filled one wall, while the others were covered with gold wallpaper that was probably once fancy but had grown old and torn. The cream-colored floors seemed like marble, the pieces arranged in square patterns. It was all fancy looking, but clearly hadn't been cared for in a long time.

Sam moved to an inner doorway, staying in the shadows close to the walls. He'd never planned on hiding inside the mansion, but now that he was there, maybe he could find Caitlin and her dad. Maybe even help them escape. But he had to move quickly before Dex and Cody came back.

Sam leaned through the doorway into a large hall. A few dim lights from another room cast creepy shadows everywhere as he tiptoed into the main entrance foyer. On one side was the front door that he'd seen Caitlin and her dad enter. A wide marble stairway with gold-colored iron railings with red velvet handrail covers rose up to the second floor on the other side of the foyer. Remembering that the man said he'd locked Caitlin and her dad upstairs, Sam quickly scampered up the first tier of steps. He didn't want to be standing in plain view if the men suddenly walked in.

At the staircase landing, two sets of stairs flowed in opposite directions to the second floor. Before he could decide which to take, he looked up and nearly lost his breath. The ceiling was painted like the sky but filled with angels, and the entire wall in front of him was stained glass. In the glass was a picture of a woman standing amidst stone columns in a colorful garden.

"Sallie Dooley," Sam muttered. It was like she was

the queen presiding over the palace. Or a ghost. He preferred to think a queen, since this was her house and he didn't like ghosts. He remembered the fancy swan bed back at Maymont that the tour guide had said was originally located at Swannanoa. Sallie Dooley must have been something else.

He picked the stairway to the right, tiptoeing into another hallway lined with doors. Which one could be holding Caitlin and Mr. Murphy? The first door was locked, but so was the next, and the next, and the next. Where could they be?

"Caitlin," he whispered as loud as he dared.

"Hello?" a voice echoed back. "Sam?"

He jerked his head in the direction of the voice. "Caitlin?"

"Sam, is that you? Can you hear me?" She sounded far away.

He backed down to the end of the hallway. "Caitlin?"

"Sam, are you there?"

He realized the voice was coming from a heating vent in the side of the wall. He bent down to the floor. "I hear you! Where are you?"

"We're locked in a room in the tower. Can you get us out?"

"I can try." He spoke into the vent, trying to keep his voice down. He glanced up to make sure no one else was coming. "Derek's gone for help. I'll try to find you."

"Sam, be careful. They have guns."

He nodded then remembered she couldn't see him. "I know. Hang on, I'm coming."

He tried to think about where the tower could be. Caitlin's voice was echoey and could be coming from anywhere in the big mansion. She couldn't be in the tower they saw in the woods since it wasn't connected to the building. He hurried to a window at the end of the hallway, craning his neck upward. There was a small stone tower extending up above the regular roofline. He suddenly remembered seeing the two towers on the building when they came in.

Sam stepped back, noticing a narrow set of stairs to the left of the window. They were built into the curve of the wall, hidden from view unless you were standing directly in front of them. Sam bolted up the winding stairs two at a time until he came to the top.

A heavy, wooden door on wide, black iron hinges blocked his path. He turned the handle, but it was locked too, so he leaned over, peeking through an old fashioned keyhole, the kind you could actually put a metal key in.

"Caitlin?"

An eye came into view on the other side of the keyhole. "Sam!"

He exhaled. "Are you okay?"

"Yeah, but Daddy's hurt," Caitlin said from behind the door. "He twisted his ankle when they pushed him up the stairs, and he can't walk very well."

"How do I get this door open?" asked Sam. He turned the handle harder but it still wouldn't budge. He looked at its heavy wooden planks and metal frame, thinking about kicking it down like they do in the movies but realized he'd probably just break his foot.

"There's a key," answered Caitlin. "That's how they locked it."

An engine rumbled closer outside. "I'll be right back," Sam promised, and then ran down the stairs to the hallway. He looked out the window again past a small balcony. The pickup truck he'd seen before was parked outside. There was just enough light from the truck to make out Cody carrying a cage from the back of the truck bed. But where was Dex?

The front door banged open. "I'm going up to check on them. I'll be right back," a voice from downstairs echoed through the hallway. Footsteps clomped up the marble stairs.

He had to hide and quick! Sam looked around, but he was trapped between the entryway stairs and the tower. Those were the only two ways out. A bead of sweat rolled down his forehead.

As the clomping steps grew louder, Sam spied a

dark, receded doorway on the other side of the hall from the tower staircase. It wasn't a great hiding spot, but it would have to do. He rushed into the shadows, pressing his back tight against the hard wood of a door. He prayed that his heartbeat, that seemed to him to be sounding like a car alarm, wouldn't be heard by Dex.

Sam held his breath as the man walked right past him through the dark hallway. It was the closest he'd been to Dex. When he turned up the tower staircase, Sam let his breath out silently. He hadn't been seen.

When Dex was out of sight, Sam crept over to the tower staircase, leaning his head around the corner just enough to see him pause at the big door at the top. Dex reached above the doorframe and then placed something in the door. The key!

"Everybody behaving themselves in here?" Dex called as he stepped into the room.

"When are you going to let us out of here?" Caitlin answered.

"Please, just let us go, we didn't mean to get in your way." That was Mr. Murphy's voice.

"I don't believe you for a second," Dex replied. "You're forgetting that we saw your little girl at Maymont. Her and the other two. Don't try to tell me that you both just wandered way up here by accident. I'm not stupid."

Sam gulped. They *had* recognized Caitlin. This was bad.

The door banged shut, sending Sam backpedaling down the stairs as he heard the key being placed back on the doorframe. He looked again for somewhere to hide. His last spot wouldn't work because the doorframe was clearly visible from the direction Dex was coming now. He was about to flee to the main stairs until he heard a voice yell from downstairs.

"Dex, let's go!"

Cody was in the foyer, he'd see him for sure that way. Sam raced back to the window at the end of the hall. The small balcony outside the window might be wide enough to hold him. The old-style window had squares of glass fitted into iron frames that split down the middle. Sam quickly raised the latch handle and the right side swung open toward him on a hinge.

He scrambled over the windowsill onto the narrow balcony. As he lowered through the window and onto the balcony, his shirt caught on the edge of the frame, yanking the glass shut. He heard the latch fall into place, locking it tight. He ducked down as he saw Dex step into the hallway.

Sam didn't dare look, but he sensed Dex standing at the window. He must have heard the bang when the window shut. Sam wondered if he was visible on the balcony if Dex looked down. He didn't move a muscle and this time counted to one hundred before carefully peering over the windowsill. Dex was gone, but the window was locked tight, with no latch on the outside to open it.

He was trapped. Again.

CHAPTER THIRTEEN

In the twilight, Sam glanced around the small balcony he was standing on, his knees pressed against the stone railing. He fit, but just barely. It was only a little bigger than a flower box, no more than one foot wide by two feet long. He was one clumsy step from falling to the stone patio below. He could just make out the ground below him through the darkness, but he tried not to think about how far down it looked.

One of the towers rose up a single story above him. He thought he could see Caitlin's shadow at the window. She must have been surprised to see him out on the ledge. She didn't call out to him, despite only being a short distance away, so he assumed the windows in the tower didn't open.

He bit his lip, trying to think. He had to do something. He couldn't sit out on the balcony all night.

That wasn't going to save anyone. He scanned the roofline, the cool air and the sounds of the forest all around him. A dark cable stretched out from the corner of the roof tiles a foot away from him, running downward at a slight angle. It looked like it headed toward the fountain in the gardens.

A thought flashed into his mind, but he didn't like it and quickly tried to push it out of his head. He remembered Derek sliding down the zip line at Maymont. Could the cable on the roof work like a zip line and get him down from the balcony? He studied it more carefully. It looked more like an old support cable than an electrical line, but it was hard to tell for sure.

He remembered his friends saying that if you touched a power line, you'd be zapped by a thousand volts. But that couldn't be right, since he'd seen birds sitting on power lines right outside Mrs. Cleary's math class plenty of times. They were often more interesting to look at than math problems, and he'd never seen the birds fry themselves. Maybe it was not touching two different power lines at once. That made more sense.

He tried to swallow the lump in his throat as he tapped the cable with one finger, jerking it back quickly in case it shocked him. His hair didn't seem to be standing on end, so he cautiously touched it again but still felt nothing. It must not be a power line.

Sam stared down at the ground, his stomach tightening. There was no way that he could jump off the ledge. This was more like one of Derek's stupid ideas than something he would usually think of.

The door creaked open below him, and Sam crouched back down against the wall.

"We're going to have to take care of them," Dex growled.

"What do you mean?" Cody answered. "It's just a dad and a little girl."

Sam inched over to the corner to see below him. In the shadows, Dex stood with his hands on his hips, looking at his partner. "I mean, take care of them. We can't afford to have any witnesses. We're almost done with this." He climbed into the pickup. Cody shook his head but followed Dex into the truck.

When the truck pulled out of sight, Sam stood up on the balcony. They must be going off to get more animals from the cottage. He had to act quickly. They could be back any minute. He tried not to think about what they had meant by "taking care of things."

Sam gripped his fingers around the cable and tugged down, testing its strength. He tried to imagine that he was jumping off the edge of the pool. That was scary to do too, but it always turned out all right. He realized as he held the metal cable that he'd never be able to slide down it without ripping the skin off his hands. He needed something to slide with.

He scanned the empty balcony then patted his empty shorts pockets. All he had was the belt for his canteen that he had thrown at the bear in the woods. He paused and considered the belt again. Maybe he could use that to slide on the cable. If it worked for James Bond or that guy in Mission Impossible, maybe it could work for him.

He pulled the belt from his waist, stretching it across the wire. He wrapped the ends around his wrists and squeezed them as tight as he could. He glanced up at the tower, wondering if Caitlin could still see him. She'd probably think his plan was stupid. Heck, *he* thought his plan was stupid, but it was the only one he could come up with. He'd always wanted to shake his fear of heights and this was as good a chance as any.

Sam stepped up on the railing, leaning on the belt stretched across the wire. This was nuts. He felt like Superman, or worse, a crazy person who thought they could fly before leaping to their death.

He saw a light bounce off the trees in the distance. They were coming back. He had to act now.

Sam closed his eyes, counted to three, then leaped off the balcony.

He was flying. At least it felt that way. He couldn't actually see anything since his eyes were closed. He didn't dare look, even in the dark. If he was falling to his death, he figured he might as well not see it coming.

He finally opened his eyes, the night air whipping by him, just in time to see a stone fountain coming right at him. Unlike the zip line that Derek rode at Maymont, this makeshift cable didn't have a stopping mechanism at the end. He was going to crash.

Sam gritted his teeth, pulled his legs up into a sitting position and braced for impact against the stone wall. Except, he didn't crash. Instead, he dropped, falling the final six feet to earth, splashing into the half-filled fountain of dirty water.

Sam shot to his feet, eager to get out of the warm, but gross, water. His hands were still wrapped in pieces of the leather belt, but it had broken in the middle, causing his fall. He tried to breathe, realizing that it could have been worse. He stared up at the balcony that he'd jumped from. It didn't look quite as high from the ground, but he was glad to be alive. He gave a wave up to the other tower, just in case Caitlin could see him.

He wished Derek had been there to watch his amazing feat. He peered off in the direction of where he'd last seen his brother depart into the woods. What was taking so long? He hoped that Dex and Cody hadn't somehow found him on their trips in the truck. Maybe they had more men standing guard at the end of the property. Or maybe Derek got lost, or fell off a cliff while wandering in the woods. Maybe he got blindsided by a distracted motorist and was lying by the side of the road...

The sound of a truck engine snapped Sam back to reality. He realized all those anxious thoughts weren't going to help him. He had to get back to the tower before Dex.

He climbed out of the fountain, dripping wet, his sneakers squeaking from being water logged. Sprinting to the back door where he'd entered earlier, Sam moved through the room with the honeycomb ceiling, into the hallway, and up the stairs. He paused briefly under Sallie Dooley's watchful eye, trying to remember which way he'd gone before on the alternating staircase.

Choosing the left set of stairs, he hustled up the steps, down the hallway, and up the narrow staircase to the tower room. Sam remembered Dex reaching over the doorway, so he stretched his arm as high as it would go up the doorframe like Dex had done, but he was too short. He tried again, putting one foot on the wall, the other on the door handle, and pushed up toward the ceiling.

"I'm coming, guys," he grunted, reaching his hand along the top of the high doorframe until his fingers landed on something metal. The key! He grabbed it, then jumped back down to the floor. He placed the key into the keyhole, and twisted the knob. The heavy wooden door swung open.

"I made it!" Sam exclaimed, bursting into the dark room. He stopped short as he realized Caitlin wasn't there. Neither was Mr. Murphy. In fact, this looked like a different room entirely. Then he saw a dark shadow, the size of a man, lying on the floor on the far side of the room.

Sam froze, realizing too late what had happened. He was in the wrong tower. He'd turned left on the staircase instead of right.

"Are you my rescue?" a man's voice asked.

Sam squinted in the darkness as the shadow stood and moved into the moonlight coming through the window. He recognized that voice. When the man's face became visible in the light, Sam gasped out loud. It was the marshal!

"Are you all right?" the marshal asked Sam who was frozen in the doorway looking dumbfounded.

Sam's mind was racing. How was this possible? "I thought you were dead!" he managed to say.

"Dead?" The marshal laughed. "Not yet, thankfully. Although I was starting to wonder if I was at the end of my rope..." He stepped over, placing his hand on Sam's shoulder. "We met in Maymont, correct?"

He nodded.

"What's your name?"

"Sam."

"Well it's good to see you, Sam," said the marshal, "but what are you doing here?"

Sam tried to focus. "We found your phone and saw the message about the eagles. We figured out the clue and came to Swannanoa to try to save them."

The marshal nodded, but looked serious. "That's some impressive detective work there, Sam, but we both need to get out of here fast."

Sam told him about how he'd seen the men drive off toward the cottage, how Derek went for help, and that Caitlin and her dad were being held in the other tower. As he finished speaking, a truck door slammed shut outside the building.

"We're too late!" moaned Sam.

The marshal went to the window and looked down. He watched for a moment, then knelt down next to Sam, looking him in the eye.

"Listen carefully, Sam. This is what I want you to do."

CHAPTER FOURTEEN

S am and the marshal hurried down the stairs from
the left tower. At the bottom, Sam went to the
other end of the hallway and up the right tower stairs
while the marshal snuck down to the foyer to locate
Dex and Cody.

Sam used the key that he'd used for the marshal's
door and turned the latch. Caitlin and her dad were
sitting in the darkness against the far wall. When Sam
entered, Caitlin jumped up and hugged him.

"You're all right! I was so worried," she gushed.

For once Sam didn't mind. He had been worried
about her too. He looked at Mr. Murphy against the
wall, his leg propped up on a chair.

"I'm happy to see you again too, Sam."

"I can't believe you zipped down that cable,"
exclaimed Caitlin.

Sam smiled. "You saw?"

Caitlin nodded. "I thought you were scared of heights."

He tried to look confident. "Yeah, well, I was desperate."

Caitlin laughed then moved alongside her dad.

"Can you walk?" Sam asked, reaching his hand to Mr. Murphy.

"I don't think I'll be running any marathons anytime soon, but I'll be okay."

Sam helped Caitlin hoist her dad up from the floor and toward the doorway. Mr. Murphy groaned as he put weight on his ankle. Sam noticed his face was flushed and he seemed to be sweating.

"We need to get you kids out of here," Mr. Murphy said.

"We *all* need to get out of here, Daddy," replied Caitlin.

Mr. Murphy nodded and looked at Sam. "Do you have a plan, or are we making this up as we go?"

Sam heard footsteps on the stairs and forced a chuckle. "Actually we have some help."

"Help?" asked Caitlin, turning her head. "Did Derek come back?"

The marshal walked into the room, causing Caitlin's jaw to drop like she'd seen a ghost.

"You're alive!" she exclaimed.

Sam put his finger to his lips, glancing down the stairs. "He was in the other tower," he whispered.

The marshal grinned. "Alive for the moment. It's good to see my fellow historian in one piece." He turned and nodded to Mr. Murphy. "Tom Drake, US Marshal's Office. Nice to meet you."

"Glad to meet you too, sir," replied Mr. Murphy. "Can you get us out of here?"

Marshal Drake nodded confidently. "We're going to try."

Sam quickly told them how he'd heard Dex saying that things were happening earlier than midnight. He couldn't tell what time it was, but he could hear the men arguing outside by the truck. They'd likely be back in the house soon.

The marshal led them cautiously down the stairs and along the hallway, Mr. Murphy limping slowly, leaning on the railing. Sam hoped they wouldn't have to make a break for it. Mr. Murphy wasn't going to be able to run very fast.

They stopped at the landing, listening for sounds of the men. There was no sign of them, but the front door was cracked open. Sam nodded silently once more to Sallie Dooley, hoping that this would be the last time he'd see her that night.

"Let's go," Marshall Drake whispered back to them, moving nimbly down the marble stairs to the front door. As the marshal peeked onto the patio, Sam's eyes wandered around the entryway. He spied several dark shadows on the floor through the doorway in the next room. He took a step toward them, but then stopped at a slight movement. He saw several sets of eyes reflecting the dim light.

"Marshal..." he whispered.

Marshal Drake walked over to where Sam stood. "Just as I thought. They're getting ready to move the animals." He stepped into the room and the others followed.

Sam glanced around. Wire cages filled with animals were everywhere. There had to be more than a dozen of them set out on the floor of the big room in two rows. None of the creatures were moving, and for a minute, Sam feared they were all dead.

He counted two eagles, which had to be the ones from Maymont, another big bird like a hawk, and an owl, but also some larger animals—a baby tiger, a bobcat, monkeys, even a small gorilla. It was unbelievable!

"Oh my gosh," whispered Caitlin. "Where did they all come from?"

Without even thinking, Sam started walking between the rows, gawking at the animals.

"There've been a rash of stolen species from collections like Maymont for several months now. Dexter and his crew tend to hit the smaller zoos to stay under the radar." The marshal gripped Sam's arm and pulled him back to the edge of the room. "Be careful. They're sedated, but let's still not get too close, okay?"

Sam gulped and nodded quickly. That sounded good to him.

"What's going to happen to all these poor animals?" said Caitlin, shaking her head. "They're so beautiful. They don't belong in tiny cages like this."

"These rare species can bring a hefty price to the highest bidder," answered Marshal Drake. "I suspect that's what's going down here tonight."

"Hefty indeed," a voice answered behind them.

Sam jumped and spun around. Dex was standing in the doorway.

"Your little friends are more resourceful than I expected, Mr. Drake."

"Let them go, Dex. This doesn't have anything to do with them," said the marshal, stiffening his stance.

"They're just kids, man," said Mr. Murphy, grimacing as he stepped forward on his bad ankle.

"Oh sure," replied Dex. "I'll just let you go. After you've seen my face and now you've seen the animals." He walked closer, a hand in his pocket. He bent in close to Sam, his breath stale like cigarettes. "I'm sure you won't tell anyone, will you now?"

"No, w-we won't," stammered Sam.

Dex let out a terrifying cackle. "Sure you won't, you little brat. Just like you didn't act on that message on the phone. Well your nosiness just cost you." He pulled a small gun out of his pocket and motioned them to the front door. "Outside. Now!"

"Daddy!" said Caitlin.

"Just do what he says," said the marshal, glaring at the gun. "They're just kids, Dex. Leave them alone."

Dex laughed again and nodded at Mr. Murphy. "He should teach his kids to mind their own business." He gestured with the gun again toward the door so they all walked outside to the patio. "Sit down. All of you."

Marshal Drake sat next to Sam, Caitlin and her dad on the step of the hard marble patio. When Cody walked around the side of the house, he eyed the row of prisoners and waved his hands at Dex. "What are you doing, man? I thought we were going to leave them locked up."

"So did I, until I found them downstairs looking at the animals."

Cody shook his head. "This is crazy, Dex."

"So what's next, boys?" said Marshal Drake. "Are you going to add murder to your growing list of felonies? Kidnapping, poaching endangered animals, theft of government property, resisting a federal officer...should I go on?"

"What about *him*, Dex?" Cody asked, nodding at

the marshal. He seemed nervous. Sam wondered if they were professional criminals or if this was their first time. He didn't know why anyone would want to steal rare animals in the first place, but he assumed the marshal was right and it was for the money. That seemed to be why most people committed crimes. At least in the movies and on TV.

"Like I told you before," said Dex, "we can't leave any witnesses."

Cody shook his head and began walking in circles. "No way, man. I didn't sign up for this." His voice grew louder. "Birds and animals are one thing, but not people. I'm not a killer."

Sam held his breath. It seemed like the two men were going to fight. He didn't know if that would help their situation or hurt it. Maybe the two of them would be distracted and they could make a run for it. He looked at Mr. Murphy, sitting next to Caitlin with his leg stretched out, and realized that probably wouldn't work.

"You should listen to your friend, Dex," called Marshal Drake. "You don't want to make this any worse than it already is."

"Shut up!" roared Dex, grabbing the marshal by the collar. He pulled him to his feet and turned toward the mansion.

"Where are you taking him?" screamed Caitlin, grabbing onto her dad's arm.

"I'm taking care of business," growled Dex. "Keep quiet or you'll be next!"

Sam gulped, his eyes growing wide. Mr. Murphy whispered to Caitlin to stay quiet and that things were going to be all right.

As Dex pushed Marshal Drake up to the front door, Cody called out. "Dex! Look at that."

Everyone turned and looked down the hill at a set of headlights rising up the driveway. Sam's mind raced. Had Derek reached the police?

Dex stopped in the doorway, then walked the marshal back to the steps. "They're here."

"They're early," said Cody.

"I told you," answered Dex. "It's show time."

CHAPTER FIFTEEN

A square, unmarked box truck pulled around the arc in the driveway, stopping next to the patio at Swannanoa. Two men wearing all black stepped out and shook hands with Dex. They looked over at the group sitting in a row.

"What's this?" asked one of the men. He was short and thin with long, dark hair pulled into a ponytail. He looked like a ninja but without any swords. The other man stayed silent, but he was big and built like the trunk of a tree. He literally didn't appear to have a neck. His head seemed to connect directly into his shoulders. Sam shuddered, imagining being squeezed to bits in those meaty hands.

"Nothing to worry about," replied Dex, coolly. "The cages are inside. Take a look for yourselves."

The two men glanced at each other then calmly stepped around the prisoners on the porch and into the mansion. Beams of light flashed through the room as they inspected the animals. After a minute, both men came back out to the truck.

"And they're all in good condition?" Ninja Man asked. No-Neck stared suspiciously, his hands at his side, ready to squeeze somebody.

"Just a tranquilizer. Should be effective for another twelve hours or so. After that, they'll be good as new." Dex gave the man a chilling smile. "Trust me."

"I don't trust anyone," hissed Ninja Man. He nodded to No-Neck, who stepped up to the truck, emerging with a silver briefcase.

Dex took the briefcase, flipping it open on the hood of the truck. Sam saw stacks of money neatly arranged inside the case.

"Very nice," said Dex, motioning to his partner. "Let's get this done."

Cody hesitated for a moment, then took another look at No-Neck and started up the steps.

Sam swallowed hard. It seemed like their opportunity to get Cody's support had faded with the arrival of the buyers.

As Cody disappeared inside the palace, a rumble sounded from further down the driveway. Ninja Man and No-Neck stopped and looked at Dex. "Another surprise?"

Dex shrugged, staring toward the sound. A single light appeared as the rumble grew closer. As it moved toward them, Sam realized it was a motorcycle. It rolled to a stop next to the truck, the rumble stopped, and two figures stepped off of the bike.

"Sorry, this is a closed party," Dex jeered, pulling the gun back out of his pocket.

Ninja Man shined his flashlight at them. It was Derek and...Mad Dog?

"Are you guys okay?" Derek asked, his nervous eyes focused on the gun.

Sam nodded. He was relieved to see his brother but feared it was too late for him and Mad Dog to help anything. Things had gone downhill fast. Now there were four bad guys instead of two. If the marshal couldn't save them, Sam feared a biker wouldn't do much better.

"What kinda party you throwing here, partner?" Mad Dog asked in his deep, gravelly voice. Even if he was only one person, he did sound tough. He looked it too, with his black leather biker pants and tattooed arms sticking out of his vest. Maybe he *could* save them after all.

No-Neck man took a menacing step forward, flexing his giant fingers.

"The kind that you're not invited to, Pops," Dex said with a sneer. "Why don't you back that bike up and pretend like you made a wrong turn. Trust me, you don't want to be here." He stepped closer to Mad Dog.

There was a pause, then Mad Dog's frown slowly turned into a smile. He chuckled and patted a worried-looking Derek on the shoulder. "You hear that? I think this dude's threatening me."

Sam shook his head at Mad Dog. This was bad. He knew Mad Dog was a tough leader of his biker gang, but this was no time to mess around. These guys meant business. If he was smart, Mad Dog would listen to Dex.

But that's when he heard it. Another rumble from down in the valley. But not like before. This was a deeper, louder rumble that echoed up the mountain like an avalanche. A light appeared up the drive. Then another. And another. Soon there were twenty lights, maybe more, streaming up the driveway toward the mansion like a swarm of fireflies shooting through the night. It was the Ghosts! Dozens of them, maybe all of them!

Ninja Man glanced at No-Neck then grabbed the money case from Dex's hand and jumped into the box truck. Sam thought he saw a hint of disappointment in No-Neck's eyes, but he turned and followed his partner into the truck. It tore off around the back of the building toward the tower, just ahead of the army of motorcycles.

"Wait!" screamed Dex. "Come back! That's *my* money!"

Sam looked up at Mad Dog. A big grin stretched across his bearded face. Derek raced over to Sam, Caitlin, and Mr. Murphy as the motorcycles formed a wide half-circle around the front of the mansion, boxing Dex and Cody in tight.

Marshall Drake walked up to Dex. "I think this party's over."

"Don't move," cried Dex, waving his gun wildly at the headlights. "I'm warning you."

"What are you going to do, shoot all of us, Dex?" The marshal reached out and grabbed the gun from Dex's grip. He handed it to Mad Dog then pushed Dex up against the patio railing. Cody quickly held up his hands in surrender before any force was required. He sat down on the patio steps, staring out at the motorcycle lights. He looked like a Christmas display all lit up.

Sam let out a long deep breath. They'd made it. Everybody was going to be okay.

Caitlin hugged her dad.

Derek high-fived Mad Dog and asked him if he could hold the gun.

"Don't get carried away, kid," Mad Dog growled with a smile.

Marshal Drake tied up Dex and Cody with some rope they found inside by the cages, securing them to the railing on the porch. He stepped up to Mad Dog. "You arrived just in time."

Mad Dog gave the gun back and shook the marshal's hand. "The name's Luke. Luke DeWitt. Derek here told us that y'all might need some assistance up here tonight. Looks like he was right."

"He sure was!" said Caitlin.

Marshal Drake nodded. "I'm mighty grateful to you."

"That was awesome!" shouted Derek.

"I didn't think you were coming back," said Sam, turning to his brother. "Think you could have taken any longer?"

Derek shrugged his shoulders. "It's not easy finding your way around in the dark, you know. Then I had to find the motel where the Ghosts were staying. It took a little time to explain to the guys that I knew Mad Dog and then for them to track him down." He put his arm around Sam. "But I'm glad you're all right, little bro. I was worried about you guys."

Mr. Murphy shook Mad Dog's hand and hugged Caitlin. "I wasn't sure how that little standoff was going to end, but I'm sure glad you came when you did."

Marshal Drake leaned up against the pickup. His face looked weary. "I've been tracking Dex for months. He's been running a smuggling ring for rare birds and animals all up and down the east coast."

"Who was he selling them to?" asked Caitlin.

"Well, those two other gentlemen that you met tonight are the middle men. They find wealthy buyers all over the world who want exotic pets that can't be bought legally on the open market."

"That's terrible," said Caitlin, pointing into the mansion. "People shouldn't have these kinds of animals as pets, they should be free in the wild. Or at least in good zoos like at Maymont."

Sam looked over at the marshal. "Why exactly were you in Maymont that day we met you?"

"I'd received a tip from an anonymous source on my phone that Dex would be making a move on the eagles, but he must have found the leak. He turned the tables and was waiting for me. They chased me through the gardens, where I bounced into you, but I didn't quite make it past the canal." He turned and looked at Dex who was sulking up on the porch. "Trust me, he's faster than he looks."

"Do you think the eagles can be returned to Maymont?" asked Derek.

"I don't see why not," replied the marshal. "They

don't seem to have been injured. They're just a little sluggish from the tranquilizer. That's the only good part about this whole scheme. The buyers won't pay for damaged goods, so the animals are kept in decent condition."

"Thank goodness," said Caitlin.

"We'll have them checked out by some professionals and hopefully get them back home soon."

Mr. Murphy stepped forward. "Speaking of getting home, I really need to get these kids back. We really appreciate everything you all have done tonight, but it's late. Boys, I'm sure your parents are going to be worried about you. I know Caitlin and I have had just about all the excitement we can handle for one day."

The marshal nodded. "I can take it from here." He looked at Mad Dog. "Think you can call the authorities for me back at your motel?"

Mad Dog nodded. "Consider it done."

"How are we going to get back to our car?" asked Sam.

Caitlin pointed down the driveway. "It's just a little ways down the road, remember?"

Derek grinned and stepped over to Mad Dog's motorcycle. "How about another ride?"

Mad Dog let out a deep chuckle. "I think that could be arranged." He turned and motioned to a few of his crewmates. They helped Sam, Derek, Caitlin, and her dad onto the back of several motorcycles. The marshal stayed behind to watch Dex and Cody and the animals until more police arrived.

And for the second time in his life, Sam rode on the back of a Harley through the night to safety.

CHAPTER SIXTEEN

S am fell asleep in Mr. Murphy's car halfway home from the Blue Ridge. He didn't think he would, with his mind so full of images from the long day, but he was exhausted. In his sleep, he dreamed about Dex pointing his gun or that the marshal was attacked by wild animals. He thought maybe it was the bobcat, escaped from its cage. Or the black bear from the Appalachian Trail.

Mr. Murphy called Mom and Dad from the car once they got within cell range to let them know they were going to be late. He didn't go into every detail, but he did give a brief overview and reported that everyone was okay.

Barely, thought Sam.

It was well after midnight when Mr. Murphy dropped them off. Mom gave them the expected hugs and a thorough look-over. Dad peppered them with questions to figure out how much of what happened was due to their mischief versus just bad circumstances. The more adventures they had, the harder it was to convince Dad that it was just coincidence.

The next morning, everyone slept in. Eventually, Sam rolled out of bed and got dressed. Hearing voices downstairs, he lazily wandered down to investigate. Mr. Haskins was sitting at the kitchen table talking to Derek while Dad drank coffee.

"Morning," said Dad. "Feel better?"

Sam nodded, sitting down in a chair. "Yeah, I was tired." He looked up at his neighbor. "Morning, Mr. Haskins."

"Not much longer," the old man grumbled, glancing at the clock. "You nearly missed it."

Sam scrunched his eyebrows together and tried to clear his brain. Even when he was wide awake it was hard to understand Mr. Haskins sometimes.

"I was just filling them in on yesterday," said Derek. He paused and grinned at Sam. "Well, most of it at least."

"Uh, huh," said Sam. He could barely believe all that had happened.

Derek's phone buzzed. "No way!" he exclaimed, staring at the screen. "Sam, check this out."

Sam took the phone from his brother. His eyes

opened wide in surprise at the screen. "Oh my gosh!" He dropped the phone on the table. It was a close-up picture of a bear. The one from the trail.

"Hey! Be careful."

"I don't want to see that," said Sam. "Once was enough for me."

Derek laughed and showed the picture to Mr. Haskins and their dad. "Mr. Murphy emailed it to me. It's the one I took with his camera."

Mr. Haskins whistled. "Ursus Americanus."

Sam turned his head. "Huh?"

"American Black Bear," replied Mr. Haskins. "Loads of 'em up there in the Blue Ridge." He glanced down at Sam over his glasses. "I told ya so."

Sam rolled his eyes. It was way too late for I-told-you-sos. Or too early.

Dad looked up, his face in a resigned expression. "Boys, just promise me one thing."

"What?" said Derek.

Dad shook his head. "Don't show this picture to your mother."

* * *

IT WAS a beautiful blue-sky morning at Maymont. Soft, puffy clouds drifted overhead as Sam and Caitlin walked down the path toward the animal habitats. It had been two weeks since their escapades in the mountains at Swannanoa. Sam was a little hesitant to be back at the place where they'd first run into the marshal and Dex, but when Caitlin called and asked them to come, he knew he couldn't miss it. It was the first morning that the bald eagles were returning to their habitat at the estate.

"I wonder if they know they're back home?" asked Sam as they walked past the black bear enclosure. He purposely kept to the far side of the path, even though the bears didn't seem to be out yet. He'd been close enough to bears lately.

"Of course they do," answered Caitlin, stepping onto the wooden bridge that led to the eagle habitat. "I told you the last time, they're very intelligent."

Sam strained to see into the fenced off area that housed the eagles. "Where are they?" he said, scanning the enclosure.

"There they are!" Caitlin pointed to the corner behind some bushes. Sam didn't see anything at first, but then one of the eagles stepped forward into the clearing. With a slight flap of its wings, it hopped up to a wooden perch. The second eagle followed, landing on a small log.

"Hi guys. Welcome back."

Both of the majestic birds swiveled their necks in Sam and Caitlin's direction.

"They're looking at us!" squealed Caitlin.

"No they're not."

"Sure they are. See?"

Sam watched the eagles closely. Their eyes blinked, but their focus stayed fixed on where he and Caitlin stood. It did kind of seem like they were watching them.

"I wonder if they remember us?" asked Caitlin.

"From Maymont before?" said Sam. "A lot of people come visit them, so I doubt it."

"No, from at Swannanoa."

Sam shook his head. "They were drugged, remember?"

"Oh, right." Caitlin leaned in toward the fence. "We helped save you," she whispered.

For a moment it looked like the first eagle leaned his head in toward them as well. Its beak opened quickly, then it stretched out its huge wings and flapped over to the far side of the habitat.

"Did you see that?" Caitlin exclaimed. "He said thank you!"

Sam rolled his eyes. "I don't know about that."

Caitlin turned and smirked at him. "Sam, sometimes things are true whether you believe them or not."

Sam considered what she said. "Like Dex hiding the animals at Swannanoa, I guess."

Caitlin grinned. "Exactly."

Sam leaned against the railing, thinking back to the mansion on Afton Mountain. He pictured the giant, stained glass window of Sallie Dooley and how everything around him now used to be her home. He stared back at the eagles.

"What are you smiling about?" asked Caitlin, glancing at him sideways.

"Nothing," said Sam. "I guess it's just good to see everyone back home."

"That's for sure," said Caitlin, turning around. "Hey, where's Derek? He said he was going to meet us down here."

They were both startled as a loud roar rang out across the lawn followed by several shouts. The noise seemed to be coming from the bear habitat.

Caitlin looked up at Sam, her mouth hanging open in surprise. "You don't think...?"

Sam sighed and shook his head as he took off toward the sound.

"Derek!"

ACKNOWLEDGMENTS

This was a fun one to write. Maymont has been on my list as a book setting for a while and was my first taste of Richmond when visiting family twelve years ago. I love finding common historical threads that can fit within the same storyline, so when I learned about Swannanoa on my own Maymont mansion tour, I knew it would make the book. Much of my research about Swannanoa was done online, but a day trip several weeks back allowed me to fact check. It's a pretty awesome place, although sadly in a partial state of disrepair. I'd definitely recommend it if you find yourself on I-64 just west of Charlottesville.

An influence for the mystery in this story was the 1956 Alfred Hitchcock thriller, *The Man Who Knew Too Much*, staring Jimmy Stewart and Doris Day. I was taken with the idea of running into a mysterious stranger and a secret hiding spot with an unusual name. It's a fun movie that should even appeal to kids 9+ if they are like mine.

As always, I have to thank my family—Mary, Matthew, Josh, and Aaron—for their patience in allowing me to use part of my spare time to create. Aaron, in particular, has turned into a great reader and ready companion for book deliveries and was the first to hear this story. Thanks to my friends in Richmond Children's Writers, especially Lana for her edits, the good folks at CHAT, bbgb books, Pat Smith at The Jefferson, Colonial Williamsburg, Lara Ivey, Sarah Takacs, Jill Tinsley, Leah Armstrong, Lucas Krost, Kim Sheard for her editing, Janie Dullard for her proofreading, and Dane at Ebook Launch for what might be my favorite cover yet.

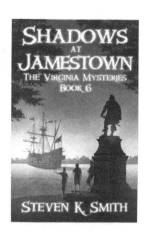

Sam, Derek and Caitlin can't believe their luck when they
are invited to help for a week on the archaeological dig at
Historic Jamestown. Maybe they'll uncover something
spectacular tracing all the way back to Captain John Smith
and Pocahontas! But when one of the priceless artifacts dug
from the Jamestown Fort is labeled a fraud, it threatens to
upend the entire project. Can the kids expose the secret
conspiracy or have they finally gotten in over their heads?
Journey back with them to America's beginnings and a
mystery in the shadows of Jamestown.

The Virginia Mysteries:

Summer of the Woods

Mystery on Church Hill

Ghosts of Belle Isle

Secret of the Staircase

Midnight at the Mansion

Shadows at Jamestown

Spies at Mount Vernon

Brother Wars

Brother Wars: Cabin Eleven

ABOUT THE AUTHOR

Steven K. Smith is the author of *The Virginia Mysteries* series and *Brother Wars* for middle grade readers. He lives with his wife, three sons, and a golden retriever named Charlie, in Richmond, Virginia.

For more information:

www.stevenksmith.net

steve@myboys3.com

CHAT

Sam, Derek, and Caitlin aren't the only kids who crave adventure. Whether near woods in the country or amidst tall buildings and the busy urban streets of a city, every child needs exciting ways to explore his or her imagination, excel at learning and have fun.

A portion of the proceeds from *The Virginia Mysteries* series will be donated to the great work of **CHAT (Church Hill Activities & Tutoring)**. CHAT is a non-profit group that works with kids in the Church Hill neighborhood of inner-city Richmond, Virginia.

To learn more about CHAT, including opportunities to volunteer or contribute financially, visit **www.chatrichmond.org.**

DID YOU ENJOY MIDNIGHT AT THE MANSION?

WOULD YOU ... REVIEW?

Online reviews are crucial for indie authors like me. They help bring credibility and make books more discoverable by new readers. No matter where you purchased your book, if you could take a few moments and give an honest review at one of the following websites, I'd be so grateful.

Amazon.com
BarnesandNoble.com
Goodreads.com

Thank you and thanks for reading!

Steve